Julie

Stacy!
Enjoy Julie.
Share with a friend.
Jane

NOVEL

Julie

JANE HOLLINGSWORTH

TATE PUBLISHING
AND ENTERPRISES, LLC

Published by Tate Publishing & Enterprises, LLC
127 E. Trade Center Terrace | Mustang, Oklahoma 73064 USA
1.888.361.9473 | www.tatepublishing.com

Tate Publishing is committed to excellence in the publishing industry. The company reflects the philosophy established by the founders, based on Psalm 68:11,
"The Lord gave the word and great was the company of those who published it."

Book design copyright © 2014 by Tate Publishing, LLC. All rights reserved.
Cover design by Allen Jomoc
Interior design by Jake Muelle

Published in the United States of America

ISBN: 978-1-63063-209-0
1. Fiction / Historical
2. Fiction / Romance / Historical / General
14.04.21

Dedication

To my daughter Joanna
To my son Glenn

Acknowledgments

I wish to thank God. This book was written with His help.

To Tate Publishing and Donna Chumley: Associate Director of Book Acquisitions, for believing in Julie. Rachael Sweeden: Director of Operations and The Book Production Team. Director of Production: Melanie Harr Hughes, Executive Editor: Curtis Winkle, Director of Marketing: Mark Mingle, Administrative Assistant: Katja Tysdal, Senior Project Manager: Stan Pearl, Lindsey Marcus, and Kate Reynolds: Project Managers, "Your book is good, let's make it better." Thank You. The Editing Department, Lay-out Department, And Design Department. Cheryl Moore: Graphic Designer and Photo Review. Special thanks to Michael and Thomas.

Chapter 1

In a small country town in the fifties, people were all about family, church, and community. Julie was born in the town of Sandy Grove, North Carolina, a pretty blond with a cute figure. She was popular with lots of friends. If you didn't like Julie, you didn't tell anyone. Her smile made you love her, and those green eyes looked into your soul. What was behind that smile and quiet confidence? What was her secret?

The popular stop for the high school students was Cox's Drugstore. The soda fountain had red stools that could spin around. Julie loved Pepsi. She and her friend Carol would drink Pepsi, talk about boys and school, but Julie never talked about her home life. She didn't invite friends home with her.

The subject with Carol today was high school graduation and the senior prom dance. The prom was next week, and Julie was going to meet Jim, a classmate, there. She was going steady with a boy that didn't go to her school. He had a job and they planned to be married. Jim was fun and made her laugh but not the type she would marry.

Julie wanted a marriage that made her feel safe and loved. She was young to be thinking about marriage, but you graduate and get married. Bryan was a good-looking man and only two years older than Julie. His job would take them to Fayetteville, only thirty five miles from Sandy Cove. Fayetteville would be their new home.

Julie planned to go to cosmetology school after graduating in May and get married in August. She would finish school in six months and work as an apprentice in a beauty salon. The apprenticeship would take another six months. Her dream was to own her salon. Her dream would come true, she had no doubt. They would build a house that she would help design. In the beginning, they would rent an apartment.

"When I start making money, then we will build our dream house." Julie said to Bryan.

Carol said, "Julie, where did you go?"

"What do you mean?"

"You were quiet and smiling.

"The future, I was thinking about my future."

"Okay, come back to the present. Do you have your dress for prom?"

"Yes. It's soft shade of pink. It's strapless with a stole."

Layers in the skirt will show how small her waist is. She didn't say this out loud. Julie didn't know she was pretty.

Carol said, "Jim wants to date you on prom night. Are you going to date him?"

Julie said, "No, I won't go to the prom with him. That wouldn't be fair to Bryan. He can't go with me. It's our class only. Maybe I could ask permission for him to come, but I don't want to. Jim and I have lots of fun together, and this may be the last time."

"Do you love Jim?"

"No, I wouldn't let myself love him, but I like him very much. Bryan is very mature for his age, and I like that."

Julie said, "Tell me about your dress and who will be your date."

"My dress is blue, and I like the way it makes my eyes shine." She had blue eyes. "No date. I had rather go alone."

"Did I tell you my dad came home Friday night with a pair of shoes for me? They have narrow straps. He heard me say I would like new shoes for my last prom."

"No!"

"I was surprised. He said the lady in the shoe store said, 'The shoes will be a hit.' I love them."

They sipped their Pepsi. When they were finished, they walked outside.

"See you at school on Monday," said Carol.

"See you."

Julie went to her daddy's car, and Carol was meeting her mom at the clothing store.

On the drive home, memories of high school came into focus. Their school only had white students. Her daddy said, "My daughter will never go to school with black children." She was never around blacks. She didn't know what the big deal was. Her mom said, "If you see one and are close, act polite." Sandy Grove had a white section and a black one. There were a few stores close to the black section. She was told never to go there and she didn't.

She wrote a short story in eleventh grade. Her teacher thought it was good. On talent night, they performed her play. Their teacher, Ms. Mills, was a great director. Every play they performed, the auditorium was full. Playing a character was easy for Julie. Being anyone but herself was nice. She was escaping.

They only had baseball and basketball at their school. In the eleventh and twelfth grade, they had a winning basketball boy's team. There were no cheerleaders, but Julie decided to change that. Ms. Mills said she would give them free time to practice.

Her grandmother didn't like the idea of her playing basketball and not too happy about cheerleading. She could help with her dad if she could sell her on the idea.

She walked into her grandmother's house and called, "Grandmama."

No one locked their door.

"I'm in the kitchen."

"Hello, Grandmama."

"What a nice surprise." She was churning milk for butter. It was a large container with a handle that she moved up and down. It was on the floor and she was sitting on a chair.

"I want to talk to you, and please don't say anything until I finish, okay?"

"Okay." She looked worried.

She told her about Ms. Mills' support and that they were the only team that didn't have cheerleaders.

Her grandmama smiled. "I will talk to your dad."

He would listen to his mother, right? He did and now Julie was a cheerleader.

After much practice and learning cheers, they were ready for basketball games.

They learned how to get the crowd involved. At halftime, they entertained the crowd with cheers. Sandy Grove's cheerleaders were a hit.

Julie lived five miles from town. Her dad always checked the mileage when she got home. He wanted to be sure she was telling the truth when she asked to drive the car. Now he knew he could trust her. She was home and her dad would want the car. He would go out drinking with his buddies but not before she left with Bryan. She would be home before her dad.

Taking time with her hair and getting dressed, she couldn't help feeling a little sad. She wished things at home could be different. She prayed that God would keep her dad safe and help her mom not to be lonely.

Her mom said, "Julie, you are pretty. Have a good time tonight. Does Bryan love you?"

"Yes, Mama."

"I want you to be happy."

"I am. Please don't worry."

Her mama left the room. Julie stood still for a minute and went into her mom's room. She was sitting by the fireplace. She didn't notice Julie. She quietly walked back to her room.

Bryan came to the door, and Julie was waiting for him. She called out, "I'll be home at eleven."

"No later than eleven," her daddy said.

"I won't."

She walked to the car with Bryan. With him she was a grown-up. They were going to dinner and to see a movie at the drive-in—dinner out, not where the food was delivered to your car; sitting at a table, not a tray on the car window. It made her feel special. Julie was careful not to kiss too much when they went to the drive-in movie. Bryan never put any pressure on her. He was happy to be dating her.

That night, when she slipped under the quilts, she was thankful to God for many things. After thinking she was in love with Joe in the tenth and some of the eleventh grade, she knew there were different kinds of love. She had prayed that God would help her meet and marry his choice for her, a man that didn't drink or need alcohol in his life. Joe drank too much. She had talked to Bryan and told him how important it was to her. He said he would have a beer with the guys at the end of the week. He agreed he wouldn't do that after they married.

Her mama was asleep, but Julie couldn't go to sleep until she heard her daddy come in. He didn't make any noise, but she heard the door close. "Thank you, God." She closed her eyes.

Sunday was a quiet day at her house. Her daddy was sleeping off the alcohol. Julie read almost every book in the school library. Her mama was concerned about her eyes. Reading took her away from the life she knew. She met and traveled with the characters in each book. Bryan would come in the afternoon but would go back to Fayetteville at night.

Julie was allowed to change the colors in her room. She had painted her walls, this time a soft shade of lavender. It always amazed her how paint could change a room. Her daddy helped with the building of their house. Until their house was finished, they rented. The last time was an apartment in a large farmhouse near railroad tracks. Julie remembered hearing the train blowing its whistle. Her daddy was proud of his craftsman house. His mother wouldn't marry his dad until he built their house. Julie loved to hear her tell the story. Her mama would tell about her daddy working his job and then coming to work on their house. Building your home was passed down to their children. "Hard work pays off," they would say. Julie dreamed about her future house with Bryan.

Her daddy always had a large garden that required Julie to help plant and harvest. She said, "When I get grown, I will never have a garden."

They had a freezer and Julie helped freeze vegetables. Her mama canned tomatoes and sauerkraut. Pigs would grow up to be ham and bacon. Their smokehouse would have meat hanging from the ceiling. They would salt hams, shoulders, and fatback. Julie learned not to make pets of those cute pigs.

Her parents grew up on farms, and owning farms was a way of passing down to each generation. It was hard work, and Julie's mom didn't want that for her daughter. Her mama and two sisters help work the farm. Her dad worked on his dad's farm too.

Julie's daddy worked at Fort Bragg, a military base. He learned the trade when he was in World War II.

Paul Butler was a proud man. When her dad was fighting in the war, Julie was home with her mom. Her dad wanted to return home. He did return but was never the same.

Her daddy would work five days, and on Friday night and Saturday, he would drink alcohol. Alcohol turns him into a different person. Julie and her mom were very quiet when he was drinking. Alcohol was the way he coped.

Julie dreaded the week-ends. She never told her friends about her home life. She loved her parents and would fight anyone who said anything. It was better that no one knew.

Her mama, sisters, along with friends, would have quilting parties. They had fun laughing loud, and as children, they wanted to know what was so funny. They were not allowed in the quilting room. They would crack the door but never heard anything that was funny. It was grown-up talk. The quilts were pretty and warm on cold nights. They would make enough quilts for each family but never sold one. Julie's mama had mental health that caused her problems. Sometimes Julie would feel like the mother. Seeing her mama at these parties was the normal times.

Chapter 2

G randmama, her dad's mom, was a good old southern Baptist. She never approved of her daddy's
choice for his wife. It caused problems in their marriage. He loved both his mother and his wife.

When Julie would stay overnight with her grandmama, she would want to put her hair in pigtails; she
hated pigtails. Her granddaddy would say, "Julie, let
her. It makes her happy." Her grandmama was always
neat. She wanted Julie to look neat too. Every morning
before breakfast, they had Bible reading and prayer. Her
granddaddy would pray, and her grandmama would
read the Bible. They had a fireplace in the kitchen
that made the meals special. These were happy times
for Julie.

Her grandparent's house had a hallway that led
through the house to the kitchen. There was a living room and bedrooms on each side of the hall and
a large screened porch on the back where her granddaddy would take a nap after lunch. At night, you could
walk by their bedroom, door ajar, and he would have his
arms around her as they were sleeping. There was love
in their house, a different kind of love.

Julie's grandmama made her pretty dresses. She was hoping that Julie would love to sew, but she never did.

One night, during revival, Julie went to church with them. She was twelve and very shy at that age. The pastor was preaching about how much God loved them and sent his son to die for them. He told about Jesus and how the children would come to him. They would sit on his lap. Jesus came as a baby and grew into a man. He told everyone about God, his father. God made each of us and he loves us. If you wanted to live with him when you die, you needed to believe he was the son of God. Julie believed and wanted to please him and live with him forever. As shy as she was, she left her grandmama and walked to the pastor. She told him she wanted to live for Jesus. The people were singing "Just as I Am."

Her grandmama was pleased, but at her house, she followed up on what the pastor said.

Julie was baptized in a river near the church. That was her inner strength through school. She had a father that loved her.

During those weekends and tough time, she was on her knees, talking to her father. God gave her a love that made it possible to believe she could do or be anything she wanted.

Julie rode the school bus, but sometimes she could drive their car. Her dad was in a carpool and drove every third week. Today, she was riding the bus. A classmate drove the bus. It was a short ride, but stopping to pick up children made the ride last longer, so Julie would read. She loved school, and seeing everyone after a long weekend was nice. All the talk today after each class would be the prom.

At school, she walked to her homeroom class. The prom would take place in the community building, a short walk from school. The teacher had a key so they could see the space. Study hall was the last period, and six were given permission to go. They would let the others know about the space.

Walking to the community building, they talked about decorating. Julie wanted cloth table covering and flowers on each table; some wanted balloons. Inside the room was empty and large. They checked closets for tables and chairs. The tables were long, but that would be okay. They planned to outline walls with tables and chairs. There would be room to dance in the center. They were talking, laughing, and began to dance with each other. Slow dance and cha-cha was fun.

One of the boys would bring records and a record player. Their prom would be simple but keeping cost down for each student. They enjoyed being together, and their time together would soon be over.

They returned to school running and not wanting to miss their bus. They planned to decorate Thursday afternoon. Her friend Jim would take her home. Jim said, "Get rid of Bryan." Julie laughed.

She walked from the bus to her house and looked at the vegetable garden. It was overgrown with weeds. Soon it would be time to clear and plant. Her daddy always had fall collards.

In her room, she removed her black-and-white oxford shoes. She untied the scarf from around her neck. The collar on the blouse was turned up. She looked in the mirror, smiling. The poodle skirt with all those slips dropped to the floor. She pulled on a pair of pedal pushers and a T-skirt. She laid on her bed and listening to her radio. The music was "Rock Around the Clock." Picking up a book, she thought, "Maybe I'll read some before homework."

"Julie," her mom called.

"Yes?"

"Do you want a Pepsi?"

"Oh, yes."

At home, she enjoyed watching wrestling with her dad on their black-and-white TV. She would always choose the one that wasn't his choice; laughing and teasing him was fun. Her mom enjoyed watching Lawrence Welch's music show with her.

On the night of the prom, Bryan surprised her by coming over around 4:00 p.m. He was able to take a few hours off from work. He wanted to take her to the prom and come back for her. She really wasn't happy, but she knew he wanted to share in her special night. Going to the beauty salon earlier was a treat. Her daddy and mama had a corsage for her.

Bryan picked her up and told her how pretty she was. He left her at the community center and said he would be back at eleven. She walked inside and was feeling free. Everyone was there and music was playing. They had dinner first. Her seat was between Jim and Carol. She didn't feel she was cheating with Jim. He was her friend. Julie laughed, danced, and yes, flirted with Jim. He didn't want her to go home with Bryan.

When she got into Bryan's car, she did feel guilty. Bryan loved her, and she was going to be his wife. She wanted to be his wife. She closed her eyes and asked God to forgive her. Julie said good night to Bryan. They would have the weekend together, Saturday night and Sunday afternoon. She went into her mama's room and, sitting on the bed, told her about the prom.

Sleep didn't come easy because she was playing the night over and over in her mind. It was a special night!

* * *

Julie was restless. Graduation was in May, a month away. She would start cosmetology school two weeks after she graduated, the next phase of her life. She was ready

Her mama was preparing her beds for flower seeds. Her flowers were always so pretty. Julie liked to see her enjoying herself.

Her daddy worked late afternoons and Saturday, getting the vegetable garden ready. Julie remembered the time she sowed peas and put too many in each hole. Her daddy told her to put three per hole. When they began to grow, he said, "Pull all but three in each hill." A lesson learned.

Late afternoon, Julie walked outside to talk to her daddy. She smiled, remembering when she told him that Bryan had asked her to marry him. It was summer.

"Why do you want to get married?"

"I love him."

"You don't know what love is. You are too young to get married."

Then he took a pail, went to the garden, and began to pick peas. After he filled the pail, he came inside.

"Julie."

"Yes, Daddy," she said, walking into the kitchen.

"Are you sure about marrying Bryan?"

"Yes."

"Does he drink alcohol?"

"No, sir." She didn't tell him sometimes he would drink a beer.

"I hope he is the right guy for you."

"Daddy, I asked God to send me the right man to marry. He saw me in Sandy Grove one day and asked who is that blond? A friend from school brought him to our house and introduced me to him. He did it the proper way. That's the way he treats me, like a lady."

She walked the rows with her daddy. He told her the potatoes were sprouting through the soil. Soon they would dig around the plants and have new potatoes. They grew a lot of potatoes, but tomatoes were his favorite vegetable. He started them from plants from the Seed and Feed Store.

"Daddy?"

"Yes."

"I will miss you."

"I will miss you too."

Chapter 3

G raduation day! Cap, gown, diploma, and practice
the walk down the aisle—she wanted it over. If
only she could get her diploma without this. *God, give
me courage.* She would have no family there, only Bryan.
Julie, think about your future with him.

Bryan came and gave her a graduation present, a
pretty dress; she couldn't believe it. She decided to wear
it. The dress was the correct size. *How did he know?*
He later shared with her about buying the dress. Bryan
said he could put two hands together and that was her
waist. He gave her height and the color of her hair.
"You can shop there after we are married," he told her.
The colors were soft pastels. She loved him; yes, she
really loved him.

She had peace and joy as she walked into school.
When she walked on stage and received her diploma,
she was smiling, not only with her lips, but on the inside.

Bryan took her to a restaurant, and they sat in a
booth. He selected a song from the player. It was "You
Belong To Me." They had a burger and held hands.
What a night.

The next day was Saturday. She showed her mom her diploma. Her daddy was in the garden.

"Julie, I can't believe you are eighteen and have finished high school. You have always been a smart girl. Are you excited about cosmetology school?

"I'm excited."

"You will ride in a carpool with your dad."

"That's okay. In August, I will live in Fayetteville and be close to school."

"I'm losing my daughter."

"I'll come home often. I'm going outside and talk to daddy. I've got to wash some clothes. Daddy and I are going to get me signed up for school Monday."

Her daddy was hoeing around each plant to keep the grass under control.

"Hello, Daddy."

"Hello." He was working in the garden and was relaxed.

"Well, my big night is over. You want to see my diploma?"

He dropped his hoe and took her diploma.

"I'm proud of you, Julie. Are we going to Fayetteville Monday?"

"Yes."

"I'll take you to lunch after you pay and sign up. You will learn the date school starts, in June?"

"Yes, in June. I'm going inside and wash my clothes."

She wished she could hear him say, "I love you." Julie couldn't remember a hug or I love you. Somehow she knew they loved her. Almost at the house, she looked back, and her dad was working again.

She stood still, remembering when the soil needed plowing. Her daddy owned a mule. Smiling, she recalled that day. Between the "Gs" and "giddyap," the poor mule didn't know what to do. After that, her daddy had someone to prepare the soil. He sold the mule. *I think that was a good decision.*

Julie wanted to see Bryan tonight, but it was getting harder to keep their kissing under control. Bryan knew she was a virgin. She had always said, "My husband will be the first." She was going to keep that promise to herself and Bryan. He knew how important their wedding night would be. He always had the strength to stop.

* * *

On Monday, Julie and her dad went to Fayetteville. She had seen the school from the outside, but today she would see the school inside. She would meet the director and owner. Her daddy would wait outside in the car. Julie was excited.

Walking through the door, she saw girls cutting and styling hair on the left. It was a large room—stations on the wall and dryers on the other wall. Straight ahead was the reception area.

"Hello, my name is Julie Butler. I have an appointment with Ms. Hill."

Julie turned and watched the girls and their clients. Hair was on the floor at one station. The hair was wet, and the stylist turned the client so she could see the back. The stylist then got a broom and was sweeping up the hair.

"Julie, will you come in my office?" asked Ms. Hill. Ms. Hill was an older lady, maybe in her fifties or early sixties. She had short hair that was styled and a pretty face with a nice smile.

"Julie, what's the reason you chose cosmetology as a career."

"Hair can really change the way a person looks. I had a neighbor that told me about a home perm when I was in the eighth grade. She said she would give me one. The soft look around my face was amazing. Later, I noticed the ends didn't look nice, so I trimmed my hair. Rolling my hair with paper also was a nice look. I cut my mom's hair and gave her a perm. My cousins were next with haircuts. I think haircuts will be my favorite part of cosmetology. The style begins with an idea and then the cut."

"Did your mom ever curl your hair with a hot iron?"

"Yes, I remembered hearing the sizzling sound and smoke. The iron would be very hot, and I was told to stand still. I would have curls, and that made my mom happy."

"You are right about haircuts. Each style must begin with a great haircut. Would you like to go on the floor and watch our stylist?"

"Yes."

"The ones you will see graduate in two weeks."

One lady had clips in her hair; another was having her hair combed.

"Julie, this is called the comb-out. She has her hair shampooed, cut, and then dried under the dryer. Come. I will show you where you will begin."

We went into another large room with mannequins on stands.

Ms. Hill told her about the book on cosmetology with one chapter per day. She would learn to pin curl on the mannequins and to shampoo each other's hair the proper way. A test on the previous chapter began each class. Practice and more practice was the way to learn.

"What do you think?"

"I can't wait to get started."

"Julie, I am excited about you."

They returned to Ms. Hill's office. Julie paid the first payment. Holding her book of cosmetology, she knew her dream was coming true. She went down the steps to the car where her dad was waiting. She was feeling excitement, purpose, and no fear.

"What do you think, Julie?"

"Ms. Hill is nice and everything is pretty. Can you believe it, Daddy? I'm going to have customers. They are called clients that will pay me to make them look pretty. Make money and enjoy my work, what more could I ask for?

Her daddy said, "I'm glad you like Ms. Hill. I want you to have fun learning."

"I will."

"Are you ready for lunch?"

"I am so hungry."

"We will go to a boarding house where the guys and I have breakfast sometimes. Also, I have talked to the owner, and you will stay there each morning until it's time for school. You will be able to walk to school and be safe with Ms. Strickland. Okay?

"Okay." She thought of how God helps his children.

The building was an old three story near the railroad tracks. Down the front hall was a large dining room. The long table with chairs in the center of the room would seat at least twenty people. Near each side wall were small tables that seated two. The wall facing the door had a large fireplace. The ceilings were twenty feet high; she was told this later.

A lady came from a door on the right and said hello to her dad.

"Kate, I want you to meet my daughter. Ms. Strickland, this is Julie."

"Kate, please. It's nice to meet you."

"It's nice to meet you, Kate."

Kate told her that the guest had a family style dinner each night. They could get to know each other. She had some guests that stayed months and some one week. It was called Kate's Boarding House.

"Sit anywhere you want to. People will be coming at twelve for lunch."

Julie wanted to sit facing the door, so she walked to one of the side tables. On each table were pretty fresh flowers, pretty table clothes, and cloth napkins. The room looked like something from *Gone with the Wind* movie. In her mind, she saw women with long dresses on the arms of tall men dressed for dinner. There was an aroma from the kitchen that made her want to sit and eat.

Kate asked her daddy, "Would you like the lunch special."

"Yes."

"Daddy, I love this. What a treat,"

"When we stop for breakfast, we eat in the room they call the country kitchen. No table clothes but the food is good."

A pretty young girl dressed in a long skirt came to their table with ice tea for Julie and coffee for her daddy. Her dad didn't drink tea. Rolls in a basket were covered with a cloth napkin.

"My name is Joyce. I will be your server."

"Thank you, Joyce." She was about her age.

Next was a plate of fried chicken, fried okra, and mashed potatoes with gravy. The servings were enough for four, not two. Her dad wasn't a big man but these were his favorite foods. Julie loved fried chicken. Everything was good. They had a choice of chocolate cake or sweet potato pie. Her mom makes the best sweet potato pie with pecans. She had cake and her dad chose the pie.

Julie and her dad having lunch would be a special memory for Julie. It wasn't only the lunch, but the time they had together.

Daddy said, "Goodbye Kate and thank you."

"Julie, when your daddy drops you off, I will have a blueberry muffin for you."

"Thank you."

Her daddy had country music on the radio, and the drive home was nice. She looked at her book on cosmetology. The first chapter was easy, but turning the pages, she knew this would be hard. She relaxed and began to sing "Sixteen Tons" with Tennessee Ernie Ford. She made her dad laugh.

She had only two weeks before starting cosmetology school.

Her friend Carol wanted her to go to Wilmington, North Carolina, and meet her aunt. She would show Julie the town. Carol planned to get a job and live with her aunt. She loved typing, so an office job was what she wanted. How could two friends be so different?

Carolina Beach was near Wilmington, and Julie loved going there. Sun bathing and watching the waves was fun.

Chapter 4

Wednesday, she would go with Carol to Wilmington but come home on Saturday morning. Bryan would take her out Saturday night. She would get her bathing suit, shirts, halter tops, and short shorts and would also take one sundress for downtown.

Carol's dad took them to Wilmington. The streets were lined with trees and two-story houses. Her aunt lived upstairs in one of those houses. She had two bedrooms, and they put their things in one. Her dad said good-bye. Her aunt was working and they were alone. They started jumping, holding hands, and singing, "Free, free at last." They went into a small kitchen, and Carol saw a note on the table.

Carol read the note to Julie,

> "Carol in the fridge is lunch for you and Julie. See you at 5:30. Have fun!"
>
> Love, Aunt Sadie

After lunch, they were walking, the sun was shining, and there was no one on the street but them. They were close to department stores and a Five and Dime store.

Julie said, "Let's look at dresses. I want a new dress for my wedding day."

"Okay."

After looking at dresses for one hour, they were bored. Julie didn't see one dress that was the one.

She had a dress in her mind but not a white one. She wanted some white lace woven into the dress. They were not having a typical wedding. She and Bryan were going to a justice of peace, and no family or friends would attend. She would let her dad know the day, but her mom would be told when they returned. They would be married in Dillon, South Carolina.

Carol said, "Let's get a Pepsi at the Five and Dime."

They sat on a stool and ordered a Pepsi.

Julie noticed that black customers ordered to go. Not one was sitting at the counter. Why?

"Julie, I'm sorry you couldn't find 'the' dress."

"I will. I'll look in Fayetteville."

They walked outside with their Pepsi. Carol had an appointment on Monday to apply for a typist. She pointed to the building and talked about the office. She would be glad when the typing test was over.

Julie told her about her visit to the school and how excited she was, lots to learn but one day at a time.

Carol said, "We need to go back to the apartment. My aunt only has one bathroom and we need to shower before she gets home." They were going to a movie. They were seeing *Country Girl* with Grace Kelly.

After the movie, Julie thought Grace Kelly was beautiful. Her hair was styled perfect for her. She wondered what it would be like to style a movie star's hair.

Carol said tomorrow was Carolina Beach day. They talked about their future, and finally, they were asleep.

They were up at 8:00 a.m. and were packing lunch and beach towels to sit on, if they were still. Carol didn't drive so Julie assumed her aunt would drive them.

At 10:00 a.m., there was a knock on the apartment door.

Carol said, "Who is that?" She looked through the peephole. "I don't believe it."

"What?"

Carol opened the door, and there stood Jim, smiling.

"Jim, what are you doing here?"

"Carol didn't tell you?"

"Carol, you knew he was coming?"

"I couldn't say no to him. Julie, he cares for you. He wants to go to the beach with us."

"Well, come in, Jim," said Julie. She was smiling. "You know I'm getting married."

"A guy can hope you will change your mind."

"You are terrible."

"I know but you like me."

"You may come with us."

"Yes!"

The three were in the front seat, and Julie was in the middle.

Julie had never kissed Jim. They would hold hands but not often. He would tease her about Bryan. She had known Jim for years in school, but in the eleventh grade, they became close friends.

He had a summer job at White lake each summer. White Lake got its name because the sand in the water was the whitest white. You could be up to your waist in the water and see the white sand. White Lake was fifteen miles from their school. It was a summer favorite to swim and ride the swings. The swings would swing in circles and high in the air. Jim operated the swings. There were other rides and hamburgers. It was a family and safe place to bring small children. High school students enjoyed it too.

"What about your summer job, Jim?"

"I won't work there this summer. I'm going into a training program."

"Where is the training program?"

"Raleigh."

It was a pretty day for the beach. Temperatures would be in the 80s. A little sun makes you prettier, or so they thought. Jim had darker skin, but Julie and Carol had pale skin. When Julie was younger, she had freckles across her nose.

"Here we are, girls."

Julie said, "Let's find a spot for our beach towels and bags."

They put their things on the sand, far enough so the water wouldn't wash over them. Carol had a book and decided to sit and read.

"Julie and I are going for a walk. Maybe we will find shells."

Julie looked at him and thought, "Why not." They walked, letting the water touch their feet. Jim reached for her hand, and Julie didn't pull away. She would miss her friend.

"Julie, you are going to school?"

"Yes, I'm excited. One day I will own a salon."

"I believe you."

"Tell me about Raleigh."

"I need to go to a larger town. My dad heard about this company, and they will train me. The training included night school. My goal is to be in management."

"I see that happening for you."

They were quiet and stopped to watch a small boy making a sandcastle with his dad. The boy had blond hair. Julie wanted a boy and girl. Job, house, and then children were their plans.

Jim turned, holding Julie's hand, and led her to the sand dunes. They sat on the sand and watched the waves. Both lost in their thoughts.

He put his arm around her waist. It was a natural thing for him to do. She hated he cared or maybe loved her. She didn't love him that way. She loved their time together. Julie said, "I love watching the waves. It is relaxing."

"I love watching you."

"Will you stop?"

"It's true, Julie. I feel complete when I'm with you."

"Jim, I think you are good looking and fun to be with."

"But?"

"I'm in love with Bryan."

"Okay, I don't want to talk about Bryan. You are my girl today."

Julie smiled at him.

"Maybe we should go and sit with Carol."

He pulled her up and touched her face. Julie and Jim were voted "best looking" in their class. Their picture was in the yearbook.

Walking back they were quiet.

Carol had put a shirt over her bathing suit. Julie had on shorts with her suit.

"Are you getting too much sun, Carol?"

"Yes, on my shoulders."

Jim took the bottle of baby oil and iodine.

"Julie, come sit. I will put some on your back."

"Okay."

He was giving gentle strokes, stopping at her neck.

Julie had her eyes closed. Then opening her eyes, she stood up.

"Thanks, Jim."

Jim didn't say anything but put the lid on the bottle. He wiped his hands on the beach towel. He had on a T-shirt and pulled it over his head. Jim was tanned and so good looking. Spreading another towel, he sat looking at the water. He had a small radio and turned it on.

Jim was called the playboy in school. He was not that way with her. The guys would tease him, "How did you get her to give you attention?" He would only smile. He was gentle and sweet with Julie.

Watching him, she was sad. "I think I have had enough sun for today. Let's go have our lunch under the shelter."

Jim turned and looked at her. He put on his T-shirt and folded the towel. He had a cooler with Pepsis. She had heard he drank beer, but she had never seen him with one. He knew Julie didn't approve of any alcohol.

She walked around where Jim was standing and turned her head so she could look into his face. She grinned at him. He smiled and the mood was broken.

"Let's eat." He sat across from Carol and Julie.

They watched people on the beach. One young man walking near the water stopped and talked to three pretty girls. There was a lady who was too big to wear a two piece suit. They were laughing and friends again.

They put trash away, and the three walked on the beach, splashing water on each other with their feet.

Julie thought, "I wish we had more time to be young and silly." The future would turn them into working adults. She ran down the beach with Jim close behind. He caught her, picked her up, and took her into the water.

"No! No!"

"You want to go under the water?"

"No, my hair will get wet."

He gently put her down, and the water was around their knees. He took her hand and they walked to the sand. Carol was watching, laughing.

"I'm to have dinner with my aunt and uncle, maybe its time to go. I'll come pick you up on Saturday." Jim was holding Julie's hand.

On the way to the apartment, they didn't talk but enjoyed the music.

It was Saturday and Julie was going home. They would leave after lunch. Carol told her the night before that she wouldn't ride home with them.

"Carol, how could you? You set me up."

"I'm sorry. Jim needs this time with you. I think in his heart, he thought he could convince you to take some time before your marriage with Bryan. I can't say I don't agree with him."

"What!"

"Julie, you had a bad relationship and then met Bryan. Are you playing it safe?"

"I want a life with Bryan. Yes, he makes me feel safe. I have prayed that God would help me find a man that was right for me. I know Bryan is that man."

"Okay. I want you to be happy. Ride home with Jim, and tell him what you told me. Please don't be mad with me."

"I'm not mad. Maybe I did need this time with Jim. I don't want to hurt him. He is special and so much fun. This isn't easy."

Lying in bed, she prayed for the right words to say.

Jim came at 1:00 P. M. Julie was ready, and he took her things to the car.

"Julie, will you forgive me?" Carol said, hugging her.

"Yes, but I'm not looking forward to the ride home."

"I wish you luck. When I get home next week after my interview, let's meet at the drugstore."

"It's a date. I had fun."

"I had fun too, Julie."

Jim was standing by the car and opened the door for her.

"Did you have fun with your aunt and uncle?"

"Yes, I saw cousins I haven't seen in months. The meal was outside. There were lots of stars, and I wanted you with me."

"Why?"

"The cool night, stars, and with all those people, I was lonely."

"I'm sorry."

"It's not your fault. I have cared for you longer than you know. I should have said something a year ago about my feelings for you."

"You not telling me made me feel more comfortable with you. I have enjoyed our time together."

They rode in silence, listening to music. Julie looked at Jim; he turned and looked at her. They didn't say anything. Can you believe the song playing was "Goodnight Irene?" They turned at the same time, smiling, then laughing.

"I will see you in my dreams."

"You will meet someone."

"Maybe I will someday."

"Do you want children?"

"Yes, only two. I have thought about a little girl that looks like you."

"I want children but not for a few years."

He stopped at a gas station. "You want a Pepsi?"

"Yes, thanks. I'm going to the ladies room."

She looked at herself in the mirror, her eyes looking back at her. The eyes are the window to the soul. She thinks about Bryan and her eyes smile.

They drink their Pepsi, and Jim keeps time to the music on the steering wheel. Julie was tapping her feet.

Finally, they drove into her driveway.

"Jim thanks for the ride home. We had fun yesterday, didn't we?"

"Yes, Julie I want you to be happy. Anytime you need me, just let me know."

"You will be happy, Jim. I will too."

He helped her take her things to the front porch. They hug and he turns to walk away but stops. He turned and looked at her. Julie waves, thinking, *Please go*. Jim walked to his car. She walked inside with tears in her eyes. Standing still, waiting to hear the car leave. *Oh Jim, I will miss you*. She looks at the clock. It was 4:00 P.M. and Bryan will be here at 7:30. Julie didn't want Bryan to know she rode home with Jim.

The weekend with Bryan was nice. He had looked at apartments in different locations and found one in the Hamont area. He wanted her to see it. It was two blocks from the bus stop. Julie would ride the bus. It would be a new adventure.

Chapter 5

S he was helping her mom with laundry so she could can cabbages, making sauerkraut. Her mom loved it. Julie wanted her clothes ready for cosmetology school. She had one more week, and then her new life would begin. She would live at home while attending school in June and July. The days will be long. She would leave early with her dad and coming home late. She would study one hour at the boarding house before school. Studying in the car would be impossible. The men talking could get loud.

On Saturday before school started, her daddy let her have the car. Carol was going to meet her at the drugstore. She will start her job the week Julie goes to school.

Carol was excited about her job. She would have some filing but mostly typing. Julie thought, "I wouldn't be excited."

Julie told her about the apartment. On Friday, Bryan was going pick her up at school and take her to see their future home. She talked about riding the city bus.

"You will ride a city bus?"

"Yes"

"Are you afraid?"

"No, it will be a twenty-minute ride. Bryan told me the area the apartment is in. It's a nice area of Fayetteville. The bus stop is a two-block walk".

"I hope you will be safe."

"I will be. I need to pick up a few things at the grocery store. Have fun at your job. Write me."

"My job will be fun, and I'll send you my mailing address. Write me."

They laughed and hugged.

She went to the grocery store and started home. She drove her daddy's car, the one she drove when she got her driving license. Her dad took the day off from work. Julie loved thinking about that day. It was her birthday.

"You ready to go get your driving license?"

"I am so ready!'

The written test was easy. She had studied. The eye test was great, but the driving test? She didn't know how to parallel park. She failed and would need to come back. There were two small towns close to Sandy Grove.

Her daddy said, "Don't be upset. We will go to Clinton, and you can take the test again."

"I don't know how to parallel park." In their small town, there was no parallel parking.

"We will practice before you go."

In Clinton, he found a space with enough room between two cars and parked.

"I'm going to stand outside and guide you. First, I want you to pull up beside the front car and back in. Use your mirrors."

He made her do it five times.

"All right, let's go get your license."

The man in the car with her made her parallel park. "You need practice but you did okay."

"I passed the driving test?"

"Yes, you did."

That was a nice man. Walking inside, she gave her dad the thumbs-up.

They walked out with Julie's driver's license.

"Do you want to drive?"

"Yes." She could see how pleased her dad was. "Thank you, Daddy."

They got a burger at a drive-in. That was a special day with her dad.

Julie smiled at the time she told her dad, "I'm quitting school." She was in the eleventh grade.

"Where will you live?"

"I want to live here with you and mama."

"I'm sorry. If you quit school, you will not live here."

"You would make me leave?"

"That's what I said. Finishing school is important."

She didn't think about quitting school again. Looking back, Julie was glad.

* * *

Julie received a letter from Carol. Carol enjoyed her job, but was attending night classes. "I think it would be more fun being the manager, what do you think Julie?" She has met a man, eight years older than her. His home is in Asheville North Carolina. "How do I know if it's love, a love that will last?" He makes me feel special, we laugh, and he is good-looking. I will let you know what I decide about love. Write to me.

Carol has only dated one boy in high school. Julie thought, *I will pray for her.*

* * *

It was Julie's first day at cosmetology school. They rode into Fayetteville. The guys were asking questions. She was glad to get to the boarding house.

Kate had a blueberry muffin and milk for her. She took her dishes to the kitchen, and Kate wanted to know if she was excited.

"Very excited, a little afraid, and what will my first day include?"

"Think of it as a journey, and travel through your day. Don't miss the little things. The big things you won't miss. Get joy out of each day."

"Thanks, I feel better. Well, my journey is beginning. I won't miss anything walking to school."

The walk wasn't long enough to calm her stomach, but she was aware of everything. The birds hopping on the grass, flowers blooming, cars passing, and people walking—Julie was taking everything in. She didn't want to think of walking through the door at school.

Inside the door, a girl was at the reception area. She asked her to sign in and remember to sign out. She told her where to put her hand bag and book. Everyone was to meet in the styling area at 8:30 a.m. The door would open to customers at 9:00 a.m.

Including Julie, nine girls were waiting for Ms. Hill in the styling area.

She told them to form a half circle.

"We will begin each day with stretching and exercise."

"What?" Julie thought to herself.

"I want you to learn that keeping your body in shape with exercise is important to your career. Try to walk twenty minutes per day. Let's begin."

They exercised for twenty minutes. Six more girls came in and began to get their stations ready for customers. They would graduate in eight weeks.

New students were taken to the back room. Peggy, a teacher, told them to get their books and find a seat. They reviewed the first chapter and told to read chapter two. They would be tested on chapter one tomorrow.

Peggy told them to meet their customers for the next eight weeks. They turned and looked at mannequins on stands. The hair was nice. Everyday, Peggy would introduce something new. That day was for making a perfect pin curl.

* * *

Bryan came to Julie's school at 5:30 p.m. on Friday. He looked at Julie with so much love in his eyes. He gave her a light kiss. They were going to see the apartment.

"If you like the apartment, I will pay a deposit and move in. The couple living there will move out the first of July." He was living with two guys and was ready to move out.

"The landlord told the couple we would be there at six. It's small, Julie. Think of it as a temporary place to live, okay?"

"Okay. I'll be in school and you working. We don't need a large place."

The area was nice with two restaurants. There was large church on the left, and Bryan turned. They passed two side streets, and he turned into a driveway. There was a center stairway. They walked up the stairs and knocked on the door to the right. A pretty girl opened the door. Bryan told her they were there to see the apartment. "I'm Bryan and this is Julie."

"Come in. I will wait downstairs in the yard."

Bryan said thank you and they walked in.

It had a small hall with three doors: one door ahead was the bath; to the right, the kitchen; and to the left, the bedroom. The kitchen was bright because of windows. It had a table with four chairs. The bath was okay. Pretty towels will make a difference. The bedroom had pull shades on two windows. The apartment was small. They would need sheets, spread, and towels. The kitchen had what they needed.

Julie put her arms around Bryan's waist and laid her head on his chest. She had to trust him with the money. She knew in her heart this was what they could afford now.

"Julie, will it work for us?"

"Yes, we will add some color with towels and placemats. You know our goal, a home that we own, and that will happen. You need to focus on your job. I need to finish school and build my client list. We will be happy here."

"I love you, Julie."

"I love you too."

She was glad to hear he would sign a three-month lease with the option to renew. Bryan worked nights one week per month. She didn't like that.

Bryan let the lady know they were leaving.

Looking up and down the street, she saw large trees and small houses. She didn't see anyone outside or on the sidewalk.

They rode in silence. Julie wanted to cry but asked God to keep her calm.

Looking at Bryan, she said, "Hi, good looking."

He turned and smiled.

"What would you like for dinner?"

"Barbecue sandwich."

"Okay."

He knew where to go. There was a drive-in on Bragg Boulevard that had good barbeque. A girl came to the car to take their order. This was one time she didn't mind the tray on the window. She wanted to be alone with Bryan.

"Bryan, is there anything new at work?" He had been with Carolina Telephone Company for one and half years.

"I was told that I would learn to install phones soon."

They had talked before, and she knew that he wouldn't work at night when he becomes an installer. He would also get a pay raise.

"You are glad?"

"Oh, yes. We can use the extra money. The more I learn, the more valuable I am to the company."

In her mind, she saw him as a manager of a department. It would happen.

They ate and rode through Fayetteville. At the market, traffic went in four directions. She knew she would enjoy living here. Shopping would be fun.

Fayetteville's original settlers were from Scotland; they arrived on the Cape Fear River in 1739. There were two fires—one in 1775, the second one during the civil war. They joined together and rebuilt both times. The oldest state university, the University of North Carolina, is in Fayetteville. Why? Julie had heard about Fort Bragg for years and wanted to know more.

Moving close to Bryan, with her head on his shoulder, the future looked bright. He loved to hear her dreams for the two of them, but now wasn't the time. Listening to music and being close was enough.

* * *

Monday during lunch break, Hilda and Julie went downtown to find a wedding dress. Gail is a new friend. She was from a small town too. There was a store called The Capital. Maybe she couldn't afford a dress there but looking would be fun.

"Oh, my, look at these pretty clothes!"

"May I help you?" A nice lady asked.

"I'm looking for a special dress."

"What size do you wear?"

"Size five."

"Petite, come this way."

While she was looking around, she thought to herself, "No, no, these won't do." *Wait, there's my dress!* Julie was holding "the" dress.

"Try the dress on." The nice lady said.

She was excited going into the dressing room with all the mirrors. She couldn't believe she found her dress.

It was a perfect fit.

"Julie, let me see."

She opened the door and stepped out.

"Wow! It'd so pretty."

She had dreamed about this dress—full skirt, fitted waist, cap sleeves, and the shade a light pink, almost white. Lace was woven through the material with three stripes at the waist. The neckline was low but not too low. Julie pulled the tag so she could see the price.

The lady said her name was Jill. "We have layaway. A small amount will hold it for you. You will have one month to pay for it."

"Will ten dollars be okay?"

"Yes."

Just like that, she had her dress.

They stopped at the Five and Dime to get a soda. Only whites were seated at the counter. Julie had noticed that in Wilmington. They watched the blacks pay for their take-outs. They got their Pepsi and walked back to school. Julie had a sandwich at school and Hilda also had one.

Hilda said, "Julie, you have your dress."

"Yes I do."

She whispered, "Are you excited about your first night with Bryan? He will be your husband."

"I am a little nervous, curious, and yes, excited."

Their lunch time was over.

* * *

Julie wrote Carol to tell her about her wedding dress.

Carol wrote Julie,

I am going steady with 'Mr. Asheville', his name is Carl. Am I in love? I think about him when I am not with him, the way he looks at me I like, and we laugh. I love to hear him say, I don't like leaving you and returning to Asheville. He wants us to live in the same town. I am not ready to leave my job and night classes.

Julie wrote Carol, don't let him pressure you. I haven't heard you say 'I love you'. Enjoy dating and ask God to give you an answer.

* * *

The weeks were passing, and her wedding day would soon come. The date was August 17. On July 1, Bryan would move into their apartment. They would ride up on the following Saturday. Bryan would buy their linens, and he wanted Julie to go with him.

The apartment was clean and ready. She had expected to help clean. They ate their takeout at their kitchen table.

Hanging towels in the bathroom, Julie said, "Bryan, these hanging are for show only.

"What?"

"These make the bathroom pretty. Get the towel you need from the cabinet."

"Yes, dear", he said, grinning.

They put their yellow tablecloths on the table. Placing a potted plant in the center with placemats on each side, Julie stood back and looked; she was pleased.

"Julie, everything has a woman's touch."

"Thanks."

They made the bed together and laid on the spread, holding hands.

While leaving, she looked back. She wanted to be with Bryan, lying close every night. This would be their first home.

"Thank you, Father, for Bryan and our future home," whispered Julie.

Bryan was locking the door. Julie moved toward him, and he took her in his arms.

Julie had already told Bryan that most cooking would be learned after she married him. He said he wasn't marrying her to be his cook. She had watched him eat. She would need to learn to cook with his help. Her instructor told her that the days in the beauty shop would be long. Cooking wouldn't be at the top of her list in the beginning.

On the third week, Julie was shampooing a real customer's hair. She wanted to style just one customer. She was told maybe next week. Sometimes, customers would request a stylist by name, and she wanted that.

After eight weeks of styling the dummies, Peggy called the owner to see her style. Combing out her style, they watched. It was soft and had a natural look.

They said, "Nice."

On Monday morning, Ms. Hill called her into the office.

"Julie, do you think you are ready to style a customer's hair?"

"I would like to try."

"That's not what I asked you."

"Yes, I'm ready to style a customer's hair."

"Today you will, but Peggy will observe. How do you feel about that?"

"Thank you. I'm excited."

The customer was nice. She talked about her daughter. She was in college.

Julie styled her first customer, and her tip was five dollars. She wanted an appointment for next week with her. "Way to go, Julie!"

After her first customer, she was allowed to style more. The days passed quickly, and then it was August 1, sixteen days until her wedding day. Her daddy wanted her to go to Sears and buy what she needed. She told him about her dress and how she paid for it.

"Tips?" he asked.

"Yes, I paid for my dress with tips." He shook his head and grinned.

* * *

Gail wanted Julie to stay overnight with her. She said her dad was gone a lot overnight; her mom told everyone it was business.

She knew he came home drunk sometimes. She couldn't help but wonder if he had another woman. Gail never talked to her mom about her dad.

Gail and one of her friends planned to pick Julie up on Sunday at lunch time. Bryan was okay with her going. She wouldn't see him on Sunday. Her single days would soon be over.

She was with Bryan Friday and Saturday night. He had talked to a friend, and on their wedding day, Julie would shower and change at their house. Her daddy would take her by their house in the morning so she could leave her things. She would go to school until lunch, and Bryan would pick her up.

Gail came by Sunday, and she had her overnight bag ready. Her friend was with her. They lived in the same neighborhood. Gail and Ann teased Julie about her wedding night.

Gail's mom was pretty. She had baked cookies. They had a sandwich and cookies.

Ann, Gail's friend, wanted to take them for a drive and go by her house. Ann had two brothers and two sisters, all younger than her. Her house was loud with laughing and talking. Julie watched, thinking, "This is what a family should be." Her mom was overweight but relaxed with all the noise. Ann introduced Julie to her mom. Then they headed for the car.

The community was small with a school. Ann and Gail had grown up there and gone to school together.

After Ann left, Gail and Julie went to her room. The house was old with high ceilings. Her room was pretty with two windows facing the street and two windows on the side. Breeze from the windows was blowing the curtains. The room had a relaxed and soft feeling with lots of white with pale pink walls. She had a picture of her mom and dad taken before Gail was born. It was a happy picture.

They played cards and then went for a walk. After dinner with her mom and younger brother, Gail and Julie laid on her bed. Hearing her talk, Julie learned she had a lonely life too. Cosmetology was her way out. She had no steady boyfriend. Julie talked about her school, friends, but very little about her home life.

* * *

She received another letter from Carol, but a short one. Carol had received a note from her sister, and in that note, "Jim was marrying a girl from Florida and moving there." How do you feel about that news Julie? Write, she says.

Julie wanted to hear from Jim but knew that wouldn't happen. They both knew that he couldn't be her friend. He loved Julie. He had been in her prayers. She wanted a girl for him, that would love and care for him. *God let this be your choice for Jim.*

She wrote and shared this with Carol.

Chapter 6

It was the night before Julie's wedding day. Lying in the room that had been hers for eighteen years, she had so many different emotions. She was sad about leaving her mom and dad. She was excited about her life with Bryan. Excitement and fear about their first night as Mr. and Mrs. Bryan Mills. Her things were packed, and her dress was hanging in a bag.

"God, I need peace. Take care of my mom and dad. Bless our marriage. Thank you."

She closed her eyes and sleep came.

Julie hugged her mom and told her, "I love you."

"Have fun with your friend, Julie."

They would come by late Sunday afternoon and tell her they were married. She couldn't share with her about marrying Bryan because she knew she would worry. Julie didn't want her day spoiled. This time, she was thinking about herself. Her mom thinking she was staying with Gail was a good idea.

Her daddy helped Julie put her things in the car. She hugged him. The guys came, and they were on their way; it was going to be a new future for her. Her daddy must have talked to them because no one talked about her marriage.

At school, one girl gave Julie a manicure; another polished her toe nails. Her hair was styled with Mrs. Hill looking on. She was having a special morning. There was a lot of teasing, and they gave her a red nightgown. At twelve, she said good-bye and met Bryan downstairs.

"Look at my girl."

"You like?"

"Oh, I like."

When they arrived at Joe's house, his wife, Marty, had a light lunch for them. The ice tea was good. They ate very little.

Julie went to the bathroom and made herself fresh. She loved her dress.

Bryan had changed his clothes at their apartment. He was handsome in his dark gray suit. His dark hair and brown eyes that twinkle with love, they were ready.

Marty took a picture.

Bryan said, "Julie, you are beautiful."

"You are handsome, and I love you."

Marty laughed. "Have fun. I know you will."

To Julie, the drive to Dillon, South Carolina, took forever. The music was nice and they didn't talk. They would start to say something and both would laugh.

Bryan said, "It won't be long, maybe forty-five minutes."

Her stomach was churning. She smiled at him. They were in Dillon, South Carolina. Bryan drove to a small white house. It had pretty flowers and green grass.

"Are you ready?" Bryan asked.

"Yes."

Bryan rang the door bell, and a lady with gray hair came to the door.

"We are Bryan and Julie." Bryan told her, smiling, "Yes, hello, Bryan and Julie."

She shook hands with Bryan and took both of Julie's hands in hers.

"I am Mrs. Russell, come in." She gave Julie a pink rose. "I will get my husband." She turned and smiled at her and walked through the door.

Julie looked around the room. Soft music was playing. She was holding Bryan's hand but didn't look up at him. Her hands were very cold but normal for her.

Mr. Russell came in. "Hello." He gave a hand shake to Bryan and a light hug for Julie.

"Julie and Bryan, why do you want to get married?"

Bryan said, "We love each other."

"Love will get you through the tough times."

"We will have tough times?" Julie thought to herself and turned to look at Bryan.

He took Julie's right hand and placed it in Bryan's right hand.

They repeated the vows that he read, smiling some and very serious sometimes. Julie saw God smiling down on them. She looked at Bryan, and when she said, "I do," she thought, "Yes I do!"

"I now pronounce you husband and wife."

Bryan took her in his arms and gently kissed her. *That's it? That wasn't so bad.*

The Russells wished them years of happiness. They signed some papers and thanked them.

In the car, she couldn't help herself. "Bryan, you are my husband." She laughed. "I'm Mrs. Bryan Mills."

He laughed, hugging her. "Julie, you are my wife."

Holding his hand with a wedding band on her finger, he had a wedding band too. They had gone together to purchase them. Bryan had to pay for both rings. One day, she would buy him a special gift.

The motel was in Myrtle Beach. He said they would have dinner before they checked in.

"So you want a rib-eye steak?"

"Yes, I am hungry." He always told her that she ate like a bird but not tonight.

Their dinner was nice with low lights and music. She enjoyed her steak. They talked too much. She was nervous, and her mind was on later. *What if he doesn't like me without clothes?* She tried to gain five pounds but no luck.

Holding her hand, they walked to the car. Bryan pulled up to the motel and said, "I'll get the key." She had stayed at a motel, maybe, three times in her life.

He took her larger bag and Julie had her makeup bag. When he opened the door, she was pleased at how pretty and clean it was. On a side table was a vase of flowers with a card.

"The flowers are pretty. Who are they from?"

"Read the card." The card read, "To my beautiful wife."

She bent over to smell because roses can have a nice fragrance. She wasn't disappointed.

"Thank you."

"You deserve flowers everyday. One day, we will have our own flower garden. That's what you said, right?"

"Yes."

"Do you want to walk on the beach?"

"I would love to. I love watching the waves. I'll change."

She took a pair of shorts and a top from the bag. She went into the bathroom and closed the door. When she came out, Bryan had changed into his shorts. After hanging their wedding clothes, they walked outside. The motel was one block from the beach.

The closer they got to the beach, the louder the sound of the ocean was. Was the ocean rough tonight? Now she could see the white caps of the waves. The stars and the moon were magic on the water. She stopped, taking in the miracle of God's work.

She looked up at Bryan, and he was looking at her. He put his arms around her, drawing her close. His kiss was soft. She dropped her hands and pulled away. He took her hand and they walked. There was no need to talk.

After walking for some time, Bryan asked, "Are you ready to go back?"

"Yes."

Bryan told her to take a shower first. Wearing her short baby doll outfit and her robe, she opened the door. Bryan smiled when she came out.

"I'll see you in a few," Bryan said, going into the bathroom.

She sat on the end of the bed, noticing that the spread and sheet were pulled down.

Bryan came out looking all man.

Gosh, she was nervous.

"I'll be back." In the bathroom, looking in the mirrors with the exhaust fan on, Julie said, "Take off your robe."

She couldn't stay in this bathroom. What will he think?

"Julie."

"Bryan."

"Yes."

"Will you turn the light off?"

"Yes."

She pushed the switch in the bathroom to off and opened the door. Bryan was sitting on the bed and got up to meet her.

"Julie, come sit on the bed." He was kneeling in front of her, holding both her hands. "I love you more than my life."

She touched his face, hair, and gave him a light kiss. She thought, "Bryan is my husband and I love him."

* * *

Riding to Wilmington, she was thinking, "I really don't want to go to his brother's house." Bryan promised her a thirty-minute drop by. They were staying overnight at Carolina Beach.

He stopped and came to open the door for her. She said, "Thirty minutes, okay?"

"I promise."

Bryan introduced her to his brother Craig and his wife Allison. They had iced tea and talked about their wedding ceremony.

Small talk wasn't easy for Julie. She was glad when Bryan said they should go.

"Come anytime, and stay overnight with us," said Allison.

Wilmington and Carolina Beach are only twenty miles away. That's how far it was from their house.

They had lunch at a small café that overlooked the sound. They saw boats and some people who were water skiing. She loved it. The sun on the water was like diamonds. There were different colors from a distance. It was pretty and she was relaxed, thinking only happy thoughts.

After lunch, they walked on the deck. Ryan asked, "Have I told you that I love you?"

"Not in the last hour. I love you too."

The motel was on the ocean front. Their room had a view of the ocean. She could see people walking on the sand, with children running ahead of their parents. *One day, Bryan and I will have children.*

"Bryan, let's walk on the beach."

"If that's what you want, let's go."

Walking and holding his hand, the future looked bright.

She looked up at Bryan and he looked at her. They stopped and he took her in this arms. What a nice feeling holding each other. They begin to walk again.

"I would like to shower before dinner."

"When you are ready, we will go back."

"Okay. Bryan, I'm so happy!"

"I always want my wife to be happy."

At dinner, she wore a sundress and Bryan in jeans and knit shirt. She wanted this to go on forever, knowing tomorrow they would go to their apartment. On Monday, Bryan would go to work, and she would go to school. They would need to stop at her daddy and mama's house. She would tell her mama she was married. *What would be her reaction?*

As they lay in bed and listened to the ocean, Bryan had his arm around her. She felt a tear on her cheek—not a sad tear, but a happy one.

On the ride to her mama's, she was quiet and talking to God. She had been so happy the last three days.

She knocked on the door. Her daddy came smiling and gave her a hug. She saw her mama.

"Hello, Mama."

"Did you have a good time with your friend?"

"Yes, I had a nice weekend. Mama, Bryan, and I got married Friday night."

"Julie!" She stood still, looking at her. Julie was smiling. "You had better be good to her, Bryan."

"I will. I promise."

She hugged Julie and hugged Bryan.

Julie, with Bryan's help, told them about the marriage, the beach, food, and how nice it was to relax. They needed to get home. Monday was a work and school day.

"Be happy, Julie," said her mama.

"I will. We will see you soon."

She was going to her new home. She was a little sad leaving them, but she wanted a new life with Bryan.

"Are you okay?"

"Yes, I'm a little sad, a married woman with grown-up responsibilities. Please give me time to learn."

"I will. We can learn together. It was hard learning to take care of myself. Now I have a wife. Let me know what you like and don't like, promise?"

"I'll try."

Driving into the driveway at their new home, Bryan didn't get out of the car.

"Julie."

"Yes?"

"I love you."

"I love you.'

He opened the door to their new home.

She smelled the clean room and everything was in place, with fresh flowers on their table. She walked over and touched them. She loved flowers. A special touch and he remembered.

"The flowers are pretty. Thank you."

"One day, we will have a yard with plants and flowers. Do you like the sound of that?"

"Yes." She thought, "One day at a time. School, job, cooking, you need to relax."

Most of her things were in the closet and drawer. She opened the closet. Her things were hanging at one end and his at the other; it was very neat. She checked out the bathroom. The towels and washcloths are in neat stacks, hanging on the towel rack, a matching set, and she loved it.

"Thank you, Bryan. Everything is neat and pretty. What are we going to have for dinner?"

"We have steaks in the fridge. I could broil us one. Will you make a salad for us?"

"I can make a salad." He had everything she needed. He had a box with rice and seasoning. They read the directions.

"The rice and steaks will be done at the same time."

She looked at him. He took a broiler pan and put the washed steaks under a hot oven broiler. The steaks smelled so good when he opened the door to turn them.

"How do you like your steak cooked?"

"No red meat for me! A little pink will be okay."

"I'll take mine out first. I want mine dark pink."

She laughed and he did too. They relaxed and ate their first meal in their first place. It was good, and they did it together. They cleaned the table and dishes. They stretched out on the bed, full and happy.

"What time do you leave for work?"

"7:15. I better not take a nap."

She liked being close to him. He had her bus schedule on the fridge for her. She would leave at 8:00 a.m.

Chapter 7

S he kissed Bryan good-bye and finished dressing. Riding the bus for twelve years, she didn't mind riding a city bus. She would review her chapter for today's lesson.

There were only five people on the bus. They made four more stops before her stop at the Five and Dime. It was 8:30 a.m., and it wasn't open. She would walk four blocks to school.

Everyone was full of questions about her weekend at school; there was a little teasing but all in fun.

Getting to work with customers was fun. The book part was hard. Diseases of the nails and scalp were boring but necessary.

She walked to her bus stop and went into the Five and Dime for a Pepsi. She was tired. Standing behind a styling chair for hours was preparing her for the salon. She was tired but pleased with her haircuts and styles. The tips were great too. She would save them and surprise Bryan with dinner and movie.

Looking at the pretty homes on her ride home was a treat. She would be home before Bryan.

She changed into shorts and set the table for dinner. Bryan was bringing takeout. She didn't care what it was but glad they were not cooking.

Bryan came in with food. She knew he was tired too.

"Go change and I will pour our tea."

"Thanks Sweetie."

When he came into the kitchen, she went to him, put her arms around his waist, looked up, and kissed him.

Hugging her, he said, "I needed that."

After dinner, they went for a walk to the corner and had ice cream.

Bryan wanted to know about her day. Was he interested or just being polite? Either one, she talked.

After taking him through haircuts and different styles, she asked about his day.

"Next week, I will work nights."

"Oh, I'll stay in our apartment alone?"

"I'll make sure you are asleep before I leave. My hours are 12:00 a.m. until 8:30 a.m."

She knew he would work nights one week each month before they married.

The week passed quickly. They were learning to share the chores. The laundry room was downstairs. Julie would put them in the washer, and Bryan would put them in the dryer and fold them together. Cooking was okay. She liked being married. Bryan said his favorite time of the day was coming home to her.

Saturday, she would go to school until twelve. Bryan would take her and pick her up. They had a date for dinner. She liked having a date with her handsome husband.

The next week when she was at the Five and Dime, this man walked up to her and called her Stella.

"My name isn't Stella."

"Why are you pretending not to be Stella?"

"Because I'm not." She moved away from him.

"I'll see you, Stella."

He was older with a beard. She didn't like the way he was looking at her.

Two weeks later, the same thing happened. This time, she was angry. She went to the counter. Her bus would arrive in ten minutes.

Maybe three weeks passed, and she didn't see him again. She was getting on the bus and heard, "Hi, Stella." Turning, she saw him. He got on the bus and sat three rows behind her. Julie's heart was racing. He would see her when she got off the bus. Would he follow her? She was at her stop, and her legs didn't want to move. The bus driver looked in the mirror.

"This is your stop."

She stood up, and she was on the street. The door closed and no one got off. She stood still until the bus was out of sight. She was shaking. The tears began to fall.

That night, she told Bryan.

He said, "You can't ride the bus again."

"What will we do?"

"I'm not sure, but for now, I'm taking you to school. I'll talk to my boss." He was holding her tight.

The next day, she told Gail and Gail told Ms. Hill.

"Julie, will you come into my office?" She went in and sat across from Ms. Hill.

"Julie, in Fayetteville, there are girls that make a living having sex with men."

With wide eyes, Julie said, "What?"

"Do you know what a prostitute is?"

"No."

"Well, I'm sure this Stella must be one. I have a friend that has a two-story house. She has an upstairs apartment that you and Bryan could rent. You can't ride the bus, but you can walk one block to school. Don't go to the Five and Dime alone anymore."

"We may not be able to afford it."

"She will rent it to you, if I ask her. Tell her what you pay now, and that will be fine with her. Do you want me to call her?

"Yes, please."

She told Bryan. They were to meet at her house at four that day. God works everything out for his children.

The apartment was nice with nine-foot ceiling, a large kitchen, a living room, bath, and a large bedroom. She loved it. After talking to her, they planned to start moving the next day.

What about our lease at our apartment?

Bryan called the landlord and he understood. He wanted one month's rent.

They had very little to move. The new apartment was nice, and they could have guests.

She let her daddy know about their new apartment. He stopped by on Monday after work. He was impressed. He gave her a letter from Carol.

"Tell mama we will come on Sunday. I will style her hair."

"I will. Be happy."

* * *

Carl and Carol are in love! They are planning a December wedding. Their home will be in Asheville North Carolina. Julie and Carol promised they would update each other each Christmas, with pictures, and so forth.

How nice the thought of receiving a Christmas card with news from a friend. *Will it be news on each Christmas?*

* * *

Bryan will go see his mom and dad, so Julie could have alone time with her mama.

On Sunday, her mama had lunch ready when they arrived. Julie helped with the dishes.

"I'll walk outside with Bryan and daddy. Rest and I will trim and style your hair."

"Okay."

Her daddy and Bryan were looking at fishing tackle. She walked around the yard. At the end of summer, the yard wasn't as pretty.

Bryan said he would see her later. She went inside and shampooed her mama's hair. Trimming her hair, she told her about school and the apartment. She wanted to know if Bryan was good to her.

"Yes, Mama, you can trust him. We do the chores together. That's good because I will be a working wife."

"Does he mind if you work?"

"No, he's proud of me."

She put her under the hair dryer. Her mama had thick brown hair. After the comb-out, Julie gave her a mirror.

"I like it."

Her daddy came in and told her, "I like your hair."

Bryan came and they drove home. He was talking about the cake his mom made. He had two pieces for them later. His mom and dad were planning to go see their place. There would be no homemade cake! *Does a husband want you to be like his mom? We are very different.* She was feeling insecure.

After dinner on Monday, they went downtown for a walk. Walking down Hay Street, this man looked at Julie. Bryan turned and yelled, "What are you looking at?"

"Bryan, what was that?"

He didn't answer.

She had never seen this side of him.

Later, she asked Bryan about yelling at the man.

"I didn't like the way he was looking at you."

"You know that could happen again. Please don't respond that way. You frighten me."

"I won't. I'm sorry."

Julie's school lessons were advancing. She had a complete knowledge of haircuts, styles, and perms. It was time for permanent hair color, touch-ups, and frosting.

Her first touch-up went well. She didn't want the color on her customer's clothes. They had told her about salon insurance to cover clothes and etc. She didn't plan to let that happened.

She was nervous about her finals and state board. She wanted to be working in a salon by November.

The first of November, Ms. Hill asked her to come in the office.

"Sit down, Julie."

"Julie, I am proud but not surprised at your ability to be a great stylist. You are great with customers too. There is a lady that has a large beauty salon and needs a new stylist. I will recommend you to her, but first, I want you to agree. She is tough, but you will be able to build a following quicker at her salon. It's in a nice area. She is coming in today. Would you like to meet her?"

"Yes."

"She expects the best from her stylist and that what you are the best. Don't ever forget that. You will get guidance to build repeat business. She is a great business woman. I will introduce you when she comes in. You have an appointment at three. The customer asked for you. Ms. Perkins is coming at 3:15. You will be cutting the customers hair, okay?"

"Okay, I will give a perfect haircut. Thank you."

Ms. Perkins watched her cut the customer's hair.

"May I have the comb, Julie?" She gave her the comb. She combed Julie's customer's hair, which was wet.

"You gave a great haircut."

Julie was to come by her salon on Saturday afternoon. She would show her around and meet the other stylists. She could make her decision then. She wanted Julie to be her new stylist. She couldn't wait to share the news with Bryan.

The salon was near restaurants and a neighborhood with large houses. Julie walked in and it was pretty. A wall separated the two sections of styling chairs. Mrs. Perkins introduced her to two stylists; the others left at lunch. Two styling chairs were at the front of the sections. One was for Mrs. Perkins and the other for Mr. Brown. She would have her styling chair on the left. She would be one of the eight stylists if she decided to come. She took her to the stock and break room.

"What do you think, Julie?"

"I would love working here."

"You finish school in November?"

"Yes, the tenth will be my last day. Then state board."

"I'll give you a break. Let's say starting the twentieth?"

"I'll be here. Thank you."

"Thank you, Julie."

Bryan was waiting in the car. She was quiet as they drove away.

"Tell me what happened."

"I got the job!"

"When do you start?"

"November 20. I will have Christmas money."

He laughed. "I'm proud of you."

"Thanks, dinner on me. I have saved tip money."

* * *

Julie's finals at school were hard—the written part. She was told Ms. Hill didn't want anyone to fail state board, so her test was tough. She was nervous about state board, and the written test. Cutting and styling her model first, helped her relax. The written test was easy compared to Ms. Hill's test. With all that behind her, she could relax.

Making dinner for her husband was fun. She wanted him to feel special. The last month had been busy for her. He was sweet and patient.

"Julie, I'm an installer and no more night work. Will you get tired of me?

Julie gave him a long kiss and said, "No. I am proud of you. You worked hard for this promotion. We can use more money, right?"

He laughs, "Yes we can."

Chapter 8

It was Julie's first day in Salon of Style. She didn't expect to have any appointments. Mrs. Perkins showed her the appointment book. She had three on the book. She knew the names. They were customers from school. She was pleased and Mrs. Perkins too.

Shampooing her first customer was like a dream come true. She was on her way. The day passed quickly, and so did the next two weeks.

Fayetteville would have a Christmas parade, and their salon would take part to represent the Cosmetology Association. Mrs. Perkins wanted Julie to be on the float with her, wearing a long gown with a mink stole. Bryan took pictures. A professional one was taken of them on the float, and it made the paper.

She was building her business, and receiving Christmas gifts from her clients was a nice surprise. Her take-home pay with some salary wasn't bad. The salary would help until she had more clients. Mrs. Perkins put her picture in the paper as a new stylist that joined her salon. That helped too.

Christmas, their first Christmas as a married couple. They were having fun buying gifts and decorating.

They made cookies to share. She enjoyed making desserts.

Bryan took her to a dress shop downtown. She tried on different dresses. She modeled each one for him, and he loved it. They decided on one, and the store owner gave them a discount. Think he enjoyed them?

They had little time for friends. With Bryan's work and hers, they had little free time. Getting to know each other and enjoying every minute they had together was enough.

They saw their families at Christmas, but they had fun with their gifts to each other. Julie gave Bryan a watch that was on layaway the month of December. He was surprised.

"I promised I would buy you a nice present one day."

He gave her a heart on a chain. It opened, and she put his and her pictures inside. They gave small gifts to each other. They were like children.

You can understand a husband and wife's love. It's hard to understand the love that God has for us. She was thankful for both.

Bryan's birthday was in January. He said no gift. They would have a steak dinner out and go to the movies. He would be twenty-two.

Her birthday was in February. Bryan surprised her with a diamond ring to go with her wedding band. Monthly payments he said, but it was paid for.

"What about no presents?"

"Julie, I wanted you to have this ring when I asked you to marry me."

"Thank you. I love it." Nineteen, married, a new career, and life is good.

Her client list was growing. She would have no more salary in March. She loved her career.

* * *

Bryan and Julie were looking at mobile homes. He showed her a park they could live in. They would buy a new mobile home. They would pay payments on their home and not on rent. They had been approved to buy.

At the end of March, they were in their new home with a fenced-in yard so Julie could grow flowers. A lady in the neighborhood said she could ride with her to work. She worked downtown.

Their mobile home was a one bedroom. Their living area was larger than a two bedroom, and everything was new and easy to keep clean. One thing Julie was afraid of was the gas stove. It would take some time before she loved that stove.

One girl that she worked with was fun. She wasn't married but engaged. They planned their lunch together. She wanted to know all about married life. Julie only had positive things to tell her. Her name was June.

There would be a hairstyling contest the first week in April. It was sponsored by the Cosmetology Association. Mrs. Perkins wanted her to enter. She was afraid. One of her customers was a good-looking woman with great hair. Julie told her about the contest.

"I will be your model."

"You will?"

"Yes, I would love too."

Her name was Joyce. She invited Julie to her home to choose a dress for the contest. Her house was big and decorated so pretty. They chose a dress that was elegant. Her hair must be just right. She would style her hair each week until the style was perfect.

Mrs. Perkins was excited that she was entering and loved the choice for her model. Each style would include a haircut at the competition. June and Mrs. Perkins were going but wouldn't enter the contest.

The night of the contest, Julie was ready. She could style and cut Joyce's hair with her eyes closed. *Ha!*

After the comb-out, their models were paraded in front of the judges. They chose three and Julie was one. They were told to stand behind their models. The trophy was large and the salon of the winner would keep it for one year. It would be on display in the salon. They called number three, number two, and the winner is Julie.

She heard claps and yelling, but she was in shock. Holding the trophy, Joyce looked up at her and winked. What a night!

The next weeks were great. There were pictures in the paper as the winner helped her business and helped the salon.

For the first time in her life, she learned about Jews. She had customers that owned stores in Fayetteville. She liked them and they liked her. She thought she had always been a good listener, but in her business, you really listen. Julie enjoyed hearing about their lives and their families.

By the end of July, she was bringing home more money than Bryan. She thought it would bother him, but no, he was proud. He told the guys he worked with. They didn't believe him, and that made him laugh.

They had never had china or silver. She had a customer who sold both. She quoted them prices, and it was a lot of money. They could have a payment plan and enjoy the items as they paid. Julie talked to Bryan, and they decided to start with china. The china was a simple pattern with a band of color with white in the center. The silver was a simple pattern also. She was excited when it came. Silver and china would be paid in full by Christmas.

Chapter 9

She didn't feel well. She had missed one period, and her stomach was queasy. Was she pregnant? They wanted children. She didn't have her second period. One night the pain was really bad, and the bleeding began. Bryan took her to the emergency room. She had a miscarriage.

Bryan took her to her mama's. She cried for their baby. She must have done something to make her miscarriage.

The doctor said on her follow-up visit, "It wasn't a healthy pregnancy, and she had done nothing wrong."

Bryan would hold her and say, "We will have children, and they will be beautiful like you."

Her mama had two miscarriages, and she understood. Bryan's brother and his wife came to see her. They had a son. They were sorry for their lost.

She was ready to go back to work. *Things happen to us and we have no control.* She could control how hard she worked. Her hours were long, and that's what she needed. She wanted to be tired, not sad.

Her mama was so sweet and wanted to wait on her.

"Mama, I need to work."

"Are you ready?"

"Yes, Mrs. Perkins has booked me appointments for Saturday morning. I'll have Sunday to rest. I'll work Monday, and Tuesday will be my day off."

Her daddy would take her home. Bryan was working. She would be there when he got home.

Seeing Bryan, she started crying.

"I'm sorry."

"Don't be sorry. I love you."

"I love you too."

He had take-out, and they had a quiet night. At work, her customers gave her a hug and said "I'm sorry." After a thank you, she changed the subject. The morning passed quickly.

On Sunday, she knew they should go to church. They had been to different ones but no home church. Bryan said they would go next Sunday.

* * *

She wanted to talk about building a house.

"We don't have land," Bryan said.

"We saw land in Pineview. Let's ask."

It's a small community about twelve miles from Fayetteville. There were two churches, a hamburger place, florist, and a post office with neat houses. It would be close to work.

"There is no for sale sign on the land."

She was not ready to give up. There was one mobile home on land with houses close by.

"Will you, next weekend, go with me and ask?"

"I promise."

She thought, "Yes."

It was Tuesday morning, and while sleeping in, the phone rang.

"Hello, Julie."

"Yes."

"Are you okay?"

"Yes, may I ask who is calling?"

"You are too pretty to be sad." It was a male voice.

She didn't say anything.

"I think about you all the time. Your husband is one lucky man."

"I'm hanging up."

"Let me talk to you."

She hung up the phone and said out loud, "This is all I need. Some nut calling me."

That night she told Bryan. He said not to worry; it wouldn't happen again. It did happen again. Bryan had been gone ten minutes, and the phone rang. On the morning of the third call, Bryan was there and told her to answer the phone. After saying hello, Bryan took the phone. Listening some and after hanging up the phone, he said, "I will take care of this. Don't you worry, I will." He was angry and left for work.

That night, she asked if he knew who was making the calls.

"Julie, I don't want to talk about it. There will be no more calls."

The way he answered her, she didn't ask anymore.

* * *

On Saturday afternoon, they rode to see the land. Bryan went to the Hamburger Hut and asked about the land. The house of the owners was close by.

"Let's stop."

"Julie, the land is not for sale."

"Bryan, please ask."

He looked at her, and she knew he would stop. They went to the door, and Bryan introduced them.

"We have a mobile home and would love to buy land. We want to build a house in the near future," Julie said.

"I have no plans to sell any more land."

"How much land does the other mobile home have?"

"They own one acre."

"Please, think about it. We want to raise our children in a small community. I love the area. It will be close to our work. It's perfect."

She smiled. "Okay. I'll think about it."

"May I see your side porch?"

"Sure."

They walked to the enclosed porch, and it was as she imagined—comfortable chairs, a table for two, and lots of books. On the way to the porch, she saw a piano.

"Mrs. Strickland, do you play the piano?"

"Yes, I teach. They come here for their lessons."

"Thank you for seeing and talking with us. May we call in two weeks?"

'Yes, you may call. It was a pleasure meeting both of you." She shook their hands.

In the car, Bryan said, "Julie, you are one saleslady."

She was on a roll in there. Did she let him say anything?

"Bryan, this will be our future home site!"

The land had lots of pine trees. They stopped and she saw their future house on the land. It had double front doors.

It was Julie's Monday off. Her day off was Tuesday. One Monday off each month gave her two days.

She walked around the mobile home park. Mrs. Dixon, the lady she rode to work with, was off on Mondays. There was a closed-in porch on the front, and she rang the bell.

"Hi, come in, Julie."

She heard, "Hello, hello" from Tweetie, her parakeet. Mrs. Dixon loved that bird. She had no children. She told her that her age was forty-one. She never wanted children. When the parakeet was sick, he went to work with her.

She closed the door to the porch. They could talk without hearing the bird.

Julie told her about the phone calls.

"Don't you think it's someone at his work?"

"I thought that too. Bryan won't talk to me about the man; the one he said wouldn't call again."

"I wouldn't push him to tell me. You know it makes him uncomfortable." She saw tears in Julie's eyes.

"Maybe you are right. Should I be afraid?"

"I would be careful. Don't go places alone."

She put her arms around Julie.

"Honey, I hope he doesn't call you again."

"Me too. Better go. I want a nice dinner for Bryan."

"Okay. See you tomorrow morning."

Julie needed someone to talk with, and Mrs. Dixon was a good listener.

Bryan was home at five thirty. Julie was setting the table with their china and silver.

Looking at her, Bryan thought, "My Julie, my beautiful Julie."

"Hello, Bryan."

"Hi, did you enjoy your day?"

"I was Mrs. Homemaker. Dinner is ready, my darling husband."

"I love you, and you are funny too." He went to wash his hands.

"Are you too tired for a movie? I need to get out."

Sometimes on her day off, she would take Bryan to work and keep the car. After one day at home, she knew how important her career was to her.

Bryan enjoyed his pot roast, rice, and gravy with a salad. He took a shower, and she washed dishes.

After his shower, smelling good, Julie put her arms around him. She kissed his cheek, placed a light kiss on his mouth, and said, "More of that later."

"Is that a promise?"

"I promise."

"I'm out of here!" Feeling free in the car, she wanted to hear about the homes and people he met today. One couple was old, and it was their first phone.

"They talked loud when I called them on their new phone. I tried to imagine us that old. Listening to them, I could see they loved each other, pictures of children, grandchildren everywhere. Are you going to grow old with me?"

"Yes, we will rock in our chairs together."

It was a special night.

At lunch, June and Julie went to Saul's for lunch. June's wedding was in October, a small ceremony with close friends and family. Julie and Bryan planned to go.

* * *

On Wednesday morning, the phone rang. Bryan has left for work.

"Hello."

"Hello, Julie."

Julie didn't say anything.

"I saw you yesterday. I like your hair. Did you and your friend have a nice lunch at Saul's Grill?"

Julie didn't answer. Her heart was pounding.

"I sure would like to take you to bed."

Julie hung up and called Bryan. She was upset, but she told him what the guy said. Bryan didn't interrupt her.

He said, "Don't cry. This will stop. I love you. See you tonight."

Mrs. Dixon picked her up, and Julie told her about the call.

"Don't you think you should report this to the police?"

"Bryan thinks he can handle the situation."

"He hasn't yet."

"I know."

The salon was empty of customers, but June was there.

"Julie, what's wrong?"

"Let's go in the back." Julie told her about the phone calls and also what Bryan said.

"Julie, I don't like this. He's watching you."

"If it is a coworker, Bryan should report it. I hope he doesn't fight. He has a temper. My customer is here. Talk later."

Bryan was waiting outside at six.

"Hi."

"Hi." He was quiet on the way home. Julie didn't mention the phone call but was hoping he would. He never did. He had their dinner, and they ate in silence.

She was tired. In the shower, the tears came. *Why? Why the calls? Why the man on the bus? Why won't Bryan talk to me?*

In bed, he turned his back to her.

"Good night, Bryan."

"Good night."

All right, now I'm mad. Julie was angry at Bryan. Talking to God would help.

"Father, I haven't done anything wrong. Help me."

There was peace and then she slept.

Next morning, he opened the door to leave with no talking, turned, and looked at her.

"Julie, I'm sorry. You are my wife and I love you. There will be no more calls."

They walked to each other, and he put his arms around her.

He never told her any details and she didn't ask. Bryan was hurting. Julie thought it was someone he works with, maybe more than that, a friend. He said no more phone calls and she chose to believe him.

At the salon, the stylists were listening to Elvis's "Don't be Cruel." They were trying to dance like him. Laughing, she joined in. Play before work.

Chapter 10

They called Mrs. Strickland about the land at Pineview.

"I have decided to sell you an acre lot. I need a down payment but no more money for one year."

Bryan said it was for tax purposes.

Mrs. Strickland said let a lawyer look over the contract. The payment made it a legal contract. In two years, the land would be paid.

The road to their house would be on Mrs. Strickland's land. In the future, she could choose to sell another lot. Their plans had a garage turning from the future road, not from the front of their house—no wasted land for a road.

October came, and the bulldozer would clear the land for the future house and their mobile home. They didn't want the bulldozer in the front yard because of the pine trees. It would be two years before they built their house. The land and mobile home would be debt-free. They would borrow money to build the house, but Bryan and Julie planned to do as much as possible. The furniture would come from the sale of the mobile home.

The next two years, they would cut trees and landscape the front for their future house.

Julie wanted to be on the land at Christmas.

Bryan said, "Maybe by your birthday."

Sometimes, the weather can slow building or anything outside. They had a great fall.

Julie's dad met them at the land on the day the water pump would be installed. The location for the pump was important.

Julie's dad said, "I will help you find water."

He found a sturdy stick in the shape of a *V*. Walking around with the stick, he said, "When the stick drops down, there is where the pump should go."

"Bryan, do you believe that?"

"I'm not sure but he does."

The man that was going to drill waited.

Her dad said, "Here, drill here."

The man didn't argue but began to drill. They had water.

"Daddy, did you make that stick drop?"

"No, the water did."

Julie smiled. Her dad was having fun.

Next weekend was the septic tank. It was now the middle of November. Their savings account would be gone. The savings in the future was for the land.

If the mobile home wasn't on the land in December, they might not be able to before spring. Snow in January or February would make it impossible to move because of the big truck.

The mobile home was moved on December 15t. It was fun watching them connect the water and septic.

It was level and everything worked. The movers were great. Julie's dad was there to enjoy the move.

Julie went to Joe's Hamburgers Hut to get food. Her dad, Bryan, and Julie had their first meal in their home on their land.

They went to worship service at the Baptist Church on the first Sunday. Everyone was nice. The music was great, and they liked the pastor. This would be their home church.

Bryan needed to talk to the pastor. He had questions. The dos and don'ts isn't what being a child of God is about.

Chapter 11

The next Saturday Bryan picked up Julie at the salon. He had been fishing with two of his coworkers, and one owned a boat.

Julie asked Bryan if he had fun and if he caught some fish.

Bryan, with a silly smile, said "Fish? Yes, we caught fish."

Julie knew something was wrong. Did she smell alcohol? Bryan was chewing gum.

Bryan was not driving the way he should. The car went off the highway.

"Bryan! Stop the car and let me drive."

"Okay." He pulled the car to the shoulder. When he got out, he was unsteady.

Julie couldn't believe he was drunk! He had broken his promise to her. The tears filled her eyes, and she drove them home.

Inside, Julie got her overnight bag. She began to put clothes into it.

"What are you doing?"

"I'm going home."

"Why?"

"Bryan, I am so disappointed in you. You broke your promise to me. No alcohol!"

"I'm so sorry. I'm sorry."

Julie didn't say anything. The tears were falling. She took her hands and lowered her face into them and cried, "Oh God, Oh God!" She went to the bathroom and put cold water on her face. Picking up her bag, she walked to the door.

"Julie, let me go with you."

"Why?"

"I love you. I can't live my life without you. This will never happen again."

"Okay, we will talk tomorrow, not today."

Bryan was asleep within ten minutes in the car. Julie was talking to God. *What am I suppose to do?* "I will never leave you." *Thank you, Father.*

Her mama wanted to know what was wrong with Bryan.

"He doesn't feel well."

Bryan fell across the bed, and she closed the door. She knew to remain calm. Years of training herself to put on a happy face would work now.

She trimmed her mama's hair, and then they made dinner together. Her daddy came home. Julie thanked God that he wasn't drunk.

"Julie, what a nice surprise."

"It was a last minute decision."

"Are you okay?"

Smiling, Julie said, "I'm fine. Bryan has had a busy week. He's taking a nap."

After sleeping for three hours, Bryan ate dinner with them.

The next day, there was silence while driving home. Bryan broke the silence.

"Julie, I promise I will never drink alcohol again."

"You promised me that before we were married."

"I know. I was a teenager again and giving into the pressure of my friends. I am ashamed, weak, without courage to say no." A tear fell on his cheek.

Tears were falling from Julie's eyes.

"I won't live in a house with anyone again that drinks. I can't and I won't."

"If I could live that time over, I would have said no thanks. Please believe me. I never want to hurt or make you unhappy."

"We won't talk about this again. I forgive you. Please call and make an appointment with the pastor. Give your life to Christ, and he will give you strength to say no."

"I promise. Julie, my love for you grows stronger everyday."

Julie couldn't believe he was being open with his feelings. It made her love him more.

"I love you, Bryan."

She took her fingers and wiped the tears from his cheeks.

Bryan called on Monday and made an appointment to see the pastor on Tuesday after work.

When he came home on Tuesday night, he said he asked God forgiveness. He told God he wanted to be his child. Bryan had listened to his dad talk about Jesus, but he said, "I didn't listen with my heart."

They hugged. Before getting into bed, they knelt and prayed together.

On Sunday, the pastor introduced Julie and Bryan to the church. Julie would move her membership next Sunday, and Bryan would be baptized. Julie had the peace she needed about their relationship to each other and to God.

Sunday was a special day. Everyone made them feel special. They had a church family.

* * *

Christmas was here. They shared small gifts. Bryan had prices for each phase of their house. Julie was more than excited. They were pleased with final phase. The architect was easy to work with. She had double front doors and two bedrooms for their children. The dream was coming true. Christmas was fun.

Bryan and Julie's birthday was dinner out. No presents. They had a plan to start their house next year on Bryan's birthday.

Julie had joined the choir. She loves to sing and get to know people. In the fall, she was asked to teach a child's class. She loved the seven- to ten-year-olds.

Their front land was almost ready for grass with its trees and soil racked smooth. The space for the house was also ready.

Working hard at their jobs and working on the land, there was very little free time. They had date night once every week. Julie liked dressing in something other than her stylist outfit.

Julie was dreaming about a baby, hoping each month it would happen. Would they have a baby? What did

Bryan think? He never talked about a baby, maybe because it made her sad.

Christmas was pretty in Fayetteville. They would ride through the town and also in subdivision to see houses with their decorations. Julie decorated their house in her mind—two wreaths made by the local florists on their double doors. Their living room would be empty of furniture, but a big tree would be in front of the large windows.

On January, they wanted to begin the foundation for their house. They planned to enjoy each phase. By the end of January, the work began. They were hoping the house would be completed by June.

The framing of their house was exciting. It was looking like a house. When the rooms were framed, Julie began to place furniture in her mind, walking from room to room. *The crib would be on this wall.* When they had a baby? "No doubts. It will happen," she told herself. She was thinking and praying.

They were choosing paint colors, tiles, and making so many decisions, and Bryan said, "That's your job." Two bedrooms would be painted and empty until she got pregnant. When the walls were ready for paint, they painted. They got prices to paint the walls, but that wasn't in the budget. They said, "Hard work won't kill us."

* * *

The pastor's wife Faye and new clients from the area wanted Julie to open a salon. The idea of having her salon was frightening.

There was a small building in Pineview that was empty. Maybe they would talk to the owners.

The house was almost completed. Julie saw the plan come alive. They were both tired. Sometimes they would stretch out on the unfurnished floor before going into the mobile home.

"Bryan, I am so happy."

"I know. Julie, we made our dream come true."

"I don't want to build another house."

"No, I love this one."

She laid her head on his chest and smiled, closing her eyes.

* * *

The mobile home was sold. They needed to shop for furniture. A new adventure!

With one half of the house empty, they moved in. They would have space, oh my, so much space.

Bryan would come home, and Julie would be sitting on the kitchen counter, waiting for him.

"What's wrong?"

"I'm afraid." she would tell him. "In the mobile home, I could see from the bedroom to the living room. There are too many rooms."

"Come here." Each time, he would put his arms around her, trying not to laugh. When he saw tears in her eyes, he said, "Julie, why are you afraid?"

"I'm not until its dark outside. Everything is so black." She hugged him and began to turn lights off room by room.

Chapter 12

In July, they were going to the beach for three days. Neighbors would watch their house.

Bryan was asked to join the telephone management team. More responsibility and a nice pay increase.

"Let's buy a new car to celebrate."

Julie was proud of him and said, "Yes."

They shopped and decided on a Mercury, their first new car. It was tan inside with leather seats, Bryan's choice. Julie enjoyed watching him with the car.

They drove their car to Carolina Beach. Walking on the beach, Julie asked Bryan, "What do you think about us having our own beauty salon?"

"I think we should go for it. Didn't you say your Fayetteville customers would drive to Pineview and support you? You have them spoiled."

"Yes, that's what they told me. I can't believe they would drive twelve miles to have their hair styled. I have loyal customers."

"When we get home, we will go see the building. I know some plumbing will be needed."

"Are you ready to paint again?"

"Yes, whatever it takes."

They put their towel on the sand. Sitting and looking at the waves was a treat. Small children were playing, and couples walking and holding hands. The ocean was amazing. Large waves pushed the water to the sand. The tide was out.

Having dinner and watching the boats, it was a nice view, and the food was good. Julie loved fried shrimp. Bryan ate shrimp and oysters.

Their weekend relaxed them.

* * *

They went to see the building that could be their beauty salon. The walls and floors were in good shape. Plumbing would be needed for the shampoo bowls. The one-half bathroom only needed cleaning and painting.

The rent was a surprise. It was low, and the first three months was lower. The owner didn't agree to help with plumbing but would supply paint.

They signed a lease, and Julie gave a two-week notice. The customers made her feel they were part of the decision. "Make sure we have our regular day and time."

A sales representative helped her with a payment plan for dryers, chairs, shampoo bowls, and units.

Bryan put a sign out: "Opening in two weeks." They were ready for business.

"Bryan, it is pretty." She looked at the soft pastel colors.

"It looks like you."

"Did I tell you a girl called and would like to work in my salon?"

"No."

"She is coming by on Monday. I will offer only commission. She has some ladies that will come with her."

"Do you have appointments for Monday?"

"Only a few, but I have a perm in the morning."

At church, they met a couple their age—William, he liked to be called Bill, and Hilda Norris. They were coming over for hamburgers on the grill that night. Hilda had grown up in Pineview. Bill had grown up in South Carolina. They were renting a house and had no children. Julie really liked Hilda.

When they arrived, Bryan had the charcoal grill on, and Julie had the hamburger patties ready. There were baked beans in the oven and a garden salad. They would have banana pudding for desert. Everyone was ready for a glass of ice tea.

Standing outside the men talking about their jobs, Julie said to Hilda, "Let's go inside."

She finished setting the table and listened to Hilda talk about their small town.

"Growing up here there was nothing, but now we have a beauty shop." She laughed.

Julie laughed too.

Bryan said, "Julie, I'm ready for the burgers."

It was nice to relax with friends. Julie had always had a close friend. They were planning a long weekend together at the beach. As Julie listened, she knew that the trip was more for the girls.

* * *

Monday came, and it was her first day in her salon. When the phone rang, and she answered, "Julie's Beauty Shop." it was real.

Julie liked Joann, the stylist. She would work three days. She was going steady and planned to marry in one year. Her hair was dark, and her smile made her pretty face light up. The customers would love her.

"God is good. He is so good to me. Thank you."

At church the following Sunday, the choir said, "Julie, we have never seen so many Cadillacs in Pineview."

Julie smiled. She was pleased with her first week.

She was busy at the beauty shop and was adding new customers. Joann and Julie had every other Monday off. It was nice having two days back to back.

A girl named Elizabeth, another stylist, wanted to work with them. Julie's plans were to stop working on Saturday. Saturday would help Elizabeth build her client business.

* * *

Bryan had joined the army reserves. Each summer, he would have two weeks of reserves. Julie would go to her parents for two nights. She missed him and didn't like the idea of staying in their home alone. In the small mobile home, she learned to, with God's help, feel safe.

Bryan was coming home from his first two weeks as an army man. She had talked to him on the phone but wanted to see him.

Dinner was ready when Bryan walked in.

"Hey, Baby!"

"Hello." She hugged and kissed his mouth, nose, and cheeks.

Bryan laughed. "Maybe I should leave more often."

"Don't think about it. You want to shower before dinner?"

"No, I'm so hungry."

He talked about the single guys in his team. They thought having fun included alcohol.

"Well, we will have a new stylist working in our beauty shop."

"You don't have enough room."

She told him how they planned to make it work. "Can you believe two weeks each month, I will have three days off?" We can plan our long weekend with Will and Hilda."

"Let me work two weeks before I take a Monday off."

"You think three nights with them will be too much?"

"Not with separate bedrooms. Will and I like to watch sports. You and Hilda can have all the beach sun you want. I'm going to take my fishing pole also. We like playing cards. I think it will be fun."

"Thanks, I know I like Hilda more than you like Will."

"Yes, that's true but I will enjoy myself."

"Good. I'm glad you are home. Maybe I will get a good night sleep."

"Are you going to take a shower?"

"No, I will soak in the tub after I clean dishes."

"I'll help."

"No, I don't need any help."

The next morning was Julie's Monday off. She had coffee in bed served by a happy-to-be-home Bryan.

* * *

Elizabeth worked with Julie on Tuesday. Her personality was more serious. Julie watched her cutting her first customer's hair, trying not to stare. She gave a nice haircut. It was important that each customer was satisfied.

Julie's Tuesday through Friday was long hours. She worked late two nights. Bryan had dinner ready both nights. He told her she was working too hard.

On Saturday afternoon, Julie would go to the beauty shop and pay bills. She wanted to watch her new hair-stylist. Joann was natural, but Elizabeth would need time to develop.

Julie wanted a baby! She didn't talk to Bryan about how often she thought of their little boy or girl. Sometimes at night, she would close the bathroom door and look out the window. The stars would shine and Julie would cry and talk to God, "Why God? I want a baby, a precious baby to love. I can't understand why you won't answer my prayers. You have blessed us and I thank you. Please, Father." She wiped her face and quietly returned to bed.

* * *

The trip to the beach with friends was fun. There were two bedrooms, a bath, and a small kitchen. They could have coffee each morning and snacks and ice tea but no cooking meals.

The first morning, Julie slipped from bed and went for a walk on the beach. She had left a note for Bryan. Being near the ocean was relaxing. Watching the sun come up and the many colors in the sky made her happy.

When she returned, everyone was having coffee. Bryan poured her a cup.

Hilda asked, "You have already walked on the beach?"

"Yes, I didn't want to wake anyone. Very few people were on the beach. It was quite and peaceful."

Julie and Hilda had planned a morning in the sun. The four would meet for lunch, doing nothing but sitting and watching the ocean. What a treat! It was a fun weekend.

* * *

In the fall, Julie was asked to work with a group of girls called Girls in Action, GA for short, in her church. She taught the girls in Sunday school. She loved them and said yes.

Julie couldn't believe it was Thanksgiving. They would go to Bryan's parents, and his brother and his wife would be there. After lunch, they would go by her parents' for cake. Driving home from their parents, she would get to enjoy the colors of fall. She wasn't disappointed; she saw yellow, bronze, brown, and orange. The drive was nice.

The salon was really busy as ladies were preparing for holiday parties and special events. The Christmas holiday was almost here.

Julie loved this time of the year because she had fun decorating the house. She knew she wanted two wreaths for her front doors. They would find the perfect tree and add to their tree decorations. Tonight they were going to Fayetteville for dinner with Will and Hilda. After dinner, they would see the streets and stores with Christmas lights and decorations. It was early December but maybe some homes would be decorated.

Their house was ready for Christmas. It was pretty from the highway. They had spot lights on their doors and Christmas lights on the tree.

The choir was having special music at Christmas. Julie loved singing the Christmas songs. The true reason for Christmas was Jesus.

Family, church, and friends made Julie and Bryan's Christmas a special one in their new house. Julie wanted to share with her dad and mama. They came and had lunch with them. Her mama thought everything was pretty. She was happy for them. Julie's daddy was so proud.

They had a light snow in February. Julie added a picture of their house to the stack.

Chapter 13

Julie wanted to go to a doctor and ask why she couldn't get pregnant. Bryan said maybe that was a good idea. She made an appointment for the first week in April.

She went to the doctor, and he could find nothing wrong. He suggested keeping a temperature chart. They did.

At the end of April, Bryan was called to active duty with the army. He would go to New Jersey.

"You are going to New Jersey without me?"

"I have no choice."

Julie began to cry, knowing he had no choice.

"Honey, they think it will be only a few months."

"Months? I don't want to be alone for months."

She talked to a few special customers about Bryan's active duty. They told her maybe after the first six weeks, she could join him in New Jersey.

"Is that possible? How can I leave my beauty shop?"

"You have two girls that will take care of us."

This was hard for Julie to believe.

"Don't worry about your customers. We aren't going to leave you. Tell Bryan to talk to someone and get their okay"

That night, Julie did talk to Bryan. He already knew she could join him, but with the business, he didn't tell her.

"Let's do it, Julie. It will make the time shorter for me. I can't believe your customers. They really love you."

"I know. We will have a new adventure in New Jersey." Julie thought, "Maybe I will return pregnant."

It was May, and Bryan would leave on Sunday. On Monday, a big vase of flowers from Bryan was delivered to the beauty shop. He placed the order before he left. When she saw them, the tears started again. She went to the bathroom and gave herself a talk. She wiped her face and came out with a smile.

Her customer asked, "Are you okay, Julie?"

"Yes, tell me about that grand baby."

Julie's motto was, "Put on a happy face." Don't let them see you hurting. She did that in school, and she would do the same now. *Six weeks and I'll be with Bryan.*

Six weeks were like six months. On her day off, she mowed grass, pulled weeds, anything to stay busy. Her dad stopped by to make sure she didn't need anything. Saturday and Sunday she stayed with her parents. Her daddy would tease her about missing him.

"You can't wait to see him. Don't you know being apart will make him love you more?"

"Do you think he misses me?"

"You know he does." Her mama said, "I have never seen anyone so in love."

Letters and phone calls helped. She shared everyday with a letter to him. Receiving love letters was something new for Bryan. He was getting teased about being lovesick. He had a framed picture of Julie with him.

He would fly home, and they would drive back. They would need their car in New Jersey. She would pack, not only for herself but casual clothes for Bryan. She was feeling like a new bride. This would be the honeymoon they never had.

Julie would give Joann more commission and make her manager until she returned.

She told Bryan that everything was covered at the beauty shop. She shared with him the details.

"Bryan, where are we going to live in New Jersey?"

"I'm going to let you help with that. I have efficiency at a motel for us until we find a place. The state is pretty. I know you will like it."

Chapter 14

New Jersey is called the Garden State, and they noticed small towns and dairy farms. Bryan told Julie he wanted to go to Atlantic City—walk on the boardwalk and see shops and the beach.

Julie loved everything about their drive. She had never traveled, and neither had Bryan. They would ride for one hour, listen to music, and not talk. Knowing each other so well, sometimes they didn't need words. Then Julie would say, "Bryan, look!" He would look and laugh. He loved her excitement.

Fort Dix was the army base, and Bryan needed to report back on Monday. He wanted to show her Trenton, which was only sixteen miles from the base.

Trenton was a city, and Julie liked small towns. Their room was very small, but Bryan promised on Monday after work, they would start looking for a place. Staying close to the base would be better for Bryan.

Driving away from the city, everything was green and fresh looking. All the houses were neat with maple trees and green lawns.

"I wish we could find a place here."

Bryan said, "I doubt we will in these neighborhoods."

They saw a park. Sitting on a bench, Julie asked about his day.

"Well, I know how to put a polished shine on my boots."

Julie laughed. "Okay, let's ride some more."

Most of the houses were older and had two stories. This street was lined with maples. "I want to live here," Julie thought.

"Look, Bryan a sign in the yard, bedroom and bath for rent."

"Julie, this will be small."

"Please stop and ask to see. I want to go into that house." It had two stories, porch on the front, and pretty shrubs and grass.

He stopped at the street, and they walked to the front door. Julie could see herself sitting in one of those rocking chairs.

A small older lady answered the door. Smiling, she said, "Yes?"

Bryan introduced them, and she said her name was Sara Hood.

Bryan said, "We saw the 'for rent' sign."

"Why would you want to rent a bed and bath?"

Bryan told her they would only be here for a few months. He gave her some background on himself and Julie.

"Julie won't have a car unless she takes me to work. She loves your neighborhood."

"How were you able to leave your business, Julie?"

Julie told her about making one stylist as manager and that she trusted her. Her customers encouraged her to go with Bryan.

"I think that is great. Would you like to see the space?"

Julie said yes.

As they walked inside, Sara told them that that was the house that belonged to her mom and dad. She grew up there. She only had one brother, and he died.

In the entry, stairs led to the second floor with a short balcony. To the right was the living room with a fireplace. The ceilings were high. Julie was guessing to herself, *Ten feet*. They passed a library with paneling and comfortable chairs; it had many books to enjoy.

"The room is upstairs."

At the top of the stairs was a hallway, and Sara turned left. She opened the door, and Julie said, "Oh, this is pretty." Walls were soft shades of blue with beddings to match. Three windows let in sunshine and a view of the yard with trees. There were shades at the windows with a swag at the top of each. The colors were blue, rose, and shades of yellow. Pillows on the bed were in the same fabric as the window treatments.

"Let me show you the bath."

The ceramic tile was in a shade of rose. The tub included a shower. The glass enclosure was frosted. The walls were rose but only a soft pale shade. The blue from the bedroom was on the window and towels.

"There is a small kitchen behind the doors in your bedroom, a under the sink refrigerator, a small stove, and sink.

"We didn't know we would have a kitchen."

"Julie, this isn't a kitchen, but for a few months, I think it will work. There is a closet on this wall. I'll let you look and talk. I'll be in the living room."

Bryan knew that Julie wanted to rent this space. Her face told him. How could he say no to that face?

Teasing her, he said, "I don't know, Julie. Can you live in this small space?"

"Yes, yes, yes!"

"Okay, let's talk to Ms. Hood."

Holding hands, they walked down the stairs.

In the living room, Ms. Hood said, "Sit."

"We would love to live here for the months we are in New Jersey." Julie was smiling and sitting on the edge of her chair.

Ms. Hood was smiling too.

"Having a young couple live in my house will bring life to this old place. I am a retired school teacher, and I miss the children. When would you like to move in?"

"Tomorrow," said Julie.

She laughed. "Don't you want to know how much to rent the space?"

Bryan answered, "Maybe we need to hear that" He laughed.

The price wasn't any more than the efficiency they were in. Julie couldn't sit still any longer. Jumping up, she pulled Bryan to his feet. She gave him a hug and light kiss.

"I guess that's a yes." Bryan walked over to Ms. Hood and she stood.

"Thank you for sharing your home with us. Everyday when I leave, I'll know Julie will be safe."

"Yes, she will be. I hope you will let me show you our area, Julie."

"I would love that. Do we need sheets and towels?"

"No, the bedding and towels are fresh and yours to enjoy."

Julie took her hand in both of hers and said, looking into her eyes, "Thank you."

"You are welcome. What time will you be here to-morrow?"

"6:00 p.m.?"

"I will see you then."

They said their good-byes and walked to the car. Julie turned and looked at the house. Ms. Hood was standing on the porch. Julie waved and Ms. Hood said, "See you tomorrow."

Driving away, Bryan said, "Julie, I'm not sure I want you in her car. Something could happen. She is old."

"No, she isn't old, older maybe. I have customers that are older, and I wouldn't be afraid to ride with them. I'll go a short distance the first time and make sure she knows how to drive, really Bryan!"

"Okay, a short trip the first time."

"Yes, honey."

There was a neighborhood store within walking distance of Ms. Hood's house.

Julie thought, "I bet they sell Pepsi."

They stopped at a grill on the way to the motel. It was a short distance from their new place. The grill had vinyl table clothes in red-and-white checks and music that they enjoyed. There was also a jukebox where you could make a new selection, and Bryan selected "True Love Ways" by Buddy Holly.

"Bryan, can you believe that we found this house and we get to live there?"

"Living my life with you always amaze me."

"Are you glad I'm here with you?"

"You know that's a yes." He reached for her hand.

His song was playing. He smiled and looked at her with those brown eyes.

He whispered, "I love you."

"I love you. I'm so happy."

The next day, they arrived at 5:55 p.m. at their apartment, and Ms. Hood was waiting for them. She opened the door.

"Welcome."

"Thank you."

"Go upstairs, and when you put away your things, come down and have something cold."

"Okay."

Bryan, after closing the door, said, "I hope we will have private time."

"We will. I think it's nice of her."

"I guess you are right."

Julie noticed fresh flowers on the chest. She touched them and guessed they came from Sara's yard. She was going to be easy to love. Getting to know her was something she was eager to do.

Putting their things in drawers and the closet was easy. It was a great place to live.

Julie went to the window and could see Sara and her brother playing as children. I hope it was a happy childhood.

"Are you ready to go downstairs?"

"Yes."

At the bottom of the stairs, Ms. Hood came from the back of the house.

"Come into the kitchen."

The kitchen ceilings were higher than the front rooms. It was bright and charming. She had a tray with lemonade, small sandwiches, and slices of cake.

"Have you eaten dinner?"

"We ate in the car, driving here."

"Then please sit and relax."

Julie thought, "I hope I don't spill or drop anything." Cloth napkins and china dishes—everything was so pretty. She planned to learn from Sara.

Bryan said, "Tell me about the store down the street. Is it a grocery store?"

"Yes and much more. The man that owns it works most days. He grew up here. He loves people. He's a deacon in his church. His name is Joseph but likes to be called Joe."

The food was really good. The cake was lemon, her mother's recipe.

"Tell me about teaching," Julie said.

"I knew at an early age I wanted to be a teacher. When I was in the fifth grade, my teacher showed us how to learn having fun. She loved us and teaching. I wanted to be like her. I enjoyed watching a student that loved to learn. It was a great reward. I only retired because of my age. Now I go to school and read to the younger children. Looking into their faces makes my day. I teach a Sunday school class every Sunday. Thank you for asking, Julie."

Bryan said, "Thank you for the goodies, but we will go upstairs. A nice hot shower will be a perfect way to end a nice evening."

"I enjoyed being with you. I hope you sleep well."

Julie wanted to hug her but decided, "Too soon. A smile and thank you for everything would be enough."

"Good night, Julie."

They went to the grocery store the previous day and decided to buy a few things. Bryan was making coffee, and Julie was cleansing her face.

"I'll have a cup of coffee and then take a shower. You know this is our honeymoon, right?"

"Yes, sweetie, I know." She came out with a clean face and walked to him, grinning. "Thank you for making me feel special."

"You are special. Come here." He pulled her on his lap and kissed her neck. He whispered in her ear, "My Julie." She kissed him, got up, and brought him his coffee.

* * *

The next morning she woke up to him kissing her good-bye.

"Are you going to work?"

"Yes, I'll call you later. Enjoy your day."

"Love you." She stretched and closed her eyes. *I'm not going to work! Today, I will check out the neighborhood store.*

Julie ate her cereal and got dressed. She wore a sun dress and sandals. She drank her coffee while looking out the window. It was a beautiful morning. She was excited about her day.

As she walked down the stairs, she thought *what and who will I find today? The house is quiet. Sara must be out. Who lives in these houses? Are they happy?* No one was on the side walk. A gentle breeze moved the leaves of the maple trees. Her days had been so full with work and the house that relaxing was a treat.

The country store was nestled under maples. There was a red door and red shutters on the two windows. The building was weathered wood; it fit the neighborhood. An old brick sidewalk led to the door.

When she opened the door, a bell made a loud sound. She thought its sound was like a cow bell. In the country, some cows wore bells around their neck. You could hear them coming.

She heard a hello before she saw anyone.

"Hello."

An older man walked from the back.

"Joe?"

"Yes, and who is this pretty girl?"

She told him her name and that she was staying in Sara's house.

"Welcome, Julie."

"I would like a cold Pepsi."

"You would like what?"

"Pepsi."

He was grinning, and she knew he liked to hear her say *Pepsi*.

"I love that southern accent."

"I have an accent?"

"You have a sweet accent." He got her a Pepsi and opened it on the old fashioned ice box bottle opener. You pull the drink forward to the opening. She had seen a box like this near her grandparent's house.

"Thank you." She reached for money in her dress pocket.

"No charge today. Tell me about yourself." He sat on a stool.

Looking at his eyes, which smiled, she told him about Bryan and herself, why they were here, and a little about their life in North Carolina.

"Do you like the mountain area or the beach in North Carolina?"

"I like both, but the beach is my favorite."

"I have been to the mountains. I went in the fall. The colors were breathtaking."

Julie wanted to hear about him.

"Tell me about this area and how long has your store been here?"

She sipped on her Pepsi as he told about the house and land that belonged to his parents.

He was an only child. He moved away after high school and joined the air force. After retiring, he and his wife moved back. They stayed with his mother until she died. His dad started the store.

"My dad died two years before I retired. The store was a blessing. I was able to keep an eye on my mom and enjoy the customers. My wife worked in a library for two years. She died one year later. I asked God, why am I here?"

"Don't you think your customers enjoy you?"

"Maybe they do."

"Do you have time to show me your yard?"

"I would love to."

He said the land was one acre big, but with the trees and mature shrubs, it appeared larger. She saw an outside swing under a large maple and beautiful daylilies of different colors on each side.

"The daylilies are so pretty."

"My wife and I started these years ago with a few plants. We divided them each spring. The beds are large because we divided and gave them food. Anytime you want to come for a Pepsi and swing, you are welcome."

"I would like that. Thank you. It was nice meeting and talking to you, Joe."

"Come again, Julie."

Julie walked away feeling sad for Joe. She hoped he would have lots of customers today.

She walked to the park but didn't stop. She would save that for another day. When she got to Sara's house, Sara was in the kitchen. "Julie, is that you?"

"Yes."

She had asked to be called Sara.

"Did you see Joe?"

"Yes, we had a nice visit. I think he is lonely."

"He is. I have him over for dinner at least once a month. Maybe he can come before you and Bryan leave. We can have dinner together."

"That would be nice."

"I have an appointment to have my haircut on Thursday. Would you like to go with me?"

"Sara, I'll cut your hair."

"I can't ask you to cut my hair."

"Yes, you can. Cutting hair is my favorite part of being a stylist."

She looked at her as if to be sure it was okay to say, "I would like to have my hair cut by Julie."

"Great. What time on Thursday?"

"At 11:00 a.m.? After you cut my hair, I will take you to lunch."

"Thank you, Sara."

She was trimming flowers for a vase. Julie watched as she arranged the flowers.

"The flowers are pretty."

"I had to buy some from the market. I had some in my yard but not enough. I'm taking them to a friend. She had surgery on her foot. Would you like to go with me?"

"She wouldn't mind?"

"No, I'll call and tell her that you are coming with me."

"I'd like that."

"Come down around 2:00 p.m., and I'll be ready."

"See you at 2:00 p.m." She went upstairs and felt so blessed. "I'm having a fun day."

At 1:55 p.m., she came down and thought, "I'm going for a short drive with Sara." Bryan will like the short part.

She would call Sara's car old. Bryan would call it a classic.

She drove out of her neighborhood, and then they were on a four-lane highway. They went about five miles, and she turned right at a signal light. They were in a newer neighborhood with smaller houses.

"Lucy lived in the country with her husband. After he died, she sold the house and ten acres. She moved because her daughter lives three miles from here."

"It's a neat neighborhood, but I like where you live better."

"Oh, so do I. This is her house." The houses were close together, but it was charming.

Sara rang the door bell, and they heard a hello.

A large lady came to the door with a walker and a boot on her foot.

"Hello, I'm Lucy. Welcome, Julie. The flowers are pretty. Thank you, Sara."

They had a nice visit. She served punch and cookies.

Saying their good-byes, they were on their way. Julie hated small talk but enjoyed learning about people. Lucy was a positive person. She was living alone and missing her husband. Her laugh was contagious.

Sara told Julie she had only known Lucy for a year. They attend the same church, and both ladies lived alone. Julie thought, "I don't want to live alone."

"You are quiet, Julie."

"I was trying to imagine living without Bryan."

"Living alone takes time to adjust. My house was built for a family, not for one old maid. I have more time for others, and that brings me joy."

"I enjoy our time together, Sara."

"You are like a fresh summer breeze. I don't doubt God brought you into my life. Meeting people isn't an accident."

Getting from the car and walking to Sara's side, she put her arms around this amazing woman. "Thanks, Sara."

"Thank you, Julie."

Tears were in Julie's eyes as she walked away.

Bryan was home, and she told him about her day. After dinner, they lay on the bed. They would watch a movie later, but now, being close was enough. Julie would like to go for a walk, but her husband needed to relax.

* * *

Thursday at 10:50 a.m., she called Sara as she walked down the stairs.

"Sara, your stylist is here."

Sara laughed. "Come in. I have already shampooed my hair."

Julie had her beauty tools and supplies.

"Sara, may I style your hair differently?"

"Yes, I trust you."

As Julie combed through her hair, she saw that she had natural wave. She was excited because she planned to make Sara a new woman.

After the comb-out, she gave Sara the mirror.

"Julie, is that me? I love it."

"You have nice hair. You are a pretty lady."

"Thank you. Are you ready for lunch?"

"Yes, let me take my things upstairs."

Julie was ready for lunch and a new adventure. The only thing Julie would criticize about Sara's driving was that she drove too slowly.

She wasn't surprised at Sara's choice for lunch. It was a small place, and as her friend would say, "This place has class." There were pretty flowers in a vase on the pale ivory table clothes and soft music with lighting that added to a relaxed lunch. When the server came, Sara asked, "Julie, may I order for you?"

"Yes." *Don't let it be fancy food*, she thought. She was hungry.

Julie listened as Sara ordered. It all sounded complicated. She chose to look around the room.

She noticed ladies, young girls, and one small girl—everyone in pretty summer dresses. Before she left with Sara, she had changed. She wore a dress with heels. Sara had changed before the comb-out. Julie noticed how she was dressed.

The small garden salad came first.

"The dressing for the salad is their house dressing. They always bring it on the side. It's good and light."

Julie always had a very small amount of dressing. She poured her dressing for her salad from a tiny white pitcher. Tasting the salad with crisp vegetables and sliced almonds, Julie thought, "Oh, this is good."

"What do you think?"

"Delicious."

"Julie, this is a tearoom. The desserts are to die for!"

Pasta sauce without meat was good. The bread was delicious. The dessert was small, and Julie was glad. It was a small piece of cake with sauce and fresh strawberries. The coffee was the end of a perfect lunch.

"Sara, this was a special treat. Everything was delicious. Thank you."

"You are welcome."

Sara moved the car from the tearoom parking lot and parked in a two hour space.

"Let's walk."

"Oh, Julie, heels." She looked at her feet.

Sara laughed.

"We aren't walking far."

Julie laughed too.

The sidewalk was on the left and a busy street was to their right. Julie saw glimpses of water. They crossed the busy street at the signal light. There was a brick walkway that led between the buildings. The walk ended and a boardwalk led in both directions. In front was a large body of water. Boats were on the water, and people were walking on the sand.

"Julie, the town of Riverwalk is built around the Hudson River. The river extends from Philadelphia to New York City."

There were benches along the sidewalk, and Sara walked over and sat down. Julie sat beside her.

"This is pretty."

"Yes, it's one of my favorite places. I wanted to share it with you."

It wasn't Carolina Beach, but it was pretty. There were lights on posts along the boardwalk.

"I bet it's pretty at night. I want Bryan to see this."

"It will make a great date. There are other places to eat. I'll give you a map of the area."

Julie liked Riverwalk. She would wear comfortable shoes when she shared the town with Bryan.

Sara talked about New York City on their drive home.

"I want to go," Julie said.

Julie told Bryan about her lunch and Riverwalk. He said they would go Saturday afternoon.

* * *

Friday after dinner, they walked to Joe's. She wanted Bryan to meet him. They talked and Julie walked outside and sat on the swing. Joe walked out with Bryan. Joe had a Pepsi in his hand. "This is for you, Julie."

"Thank you."

"This is the first time I saw you sitting in my swing. Why haven't I seen you?"

"I have been busy with Sara. She is showing me the area." She told him about Riverwalk.

"She can't have all your time." He grinned at her.

Bryan asked him about his house. Joe loved talking about his place.

They said good-bye.

"Do you like Joe?"

"Yes. He is lonely. We will go again."

On Saturday, they went to Riverwalk. With Sara's map, they saw pretty homes, neat shops, and had lunch at a riverfront café. After lunch, they went into a shop that sold items for the home. Julie saw many things she liked, but maybe she'll purchase some in the future, not now.

Bryan told her the afternoon was fun because he was with her. They were sitting on a bench at the river.

"We have been busy planning our house and the beauty shop. I'm glad we reached our goals, but now it's just you and me. This is nice."

"I agree." She had enjoyed today with Bryan. They had an early dinner at Martin's Steak House. The rib eye steak was good, and the dining room was romantic. The waiter was a young man, and he told them that a live show would begin at 6:00 p.m. Bryan ordered coffee and dessert so they could stay. The music was pretty with guitars and drums. The beat was beach music. The '50s music was great.

While holding hands and walking to their car, Julie stopped and looked at Bryan.

"Bryan, we had a great date, dinner, and live music. I loved it."

"We will have more dates. I promise."

Chapter 15

Julie had two weeks of vacation but was feeling rest-less. There wasn't enough to keep her busy. She wrote letters to her mom and dad. She called the beauty salon and went with Sara to different places. She walked to Joe's and talked. Bryan couldn't tell her when they would go home. He loved their life in New Jersey. Julie missed their house and the beauty shop.

They were planning a trip to New York City with Sara. Bryan would drive, but Sara would give directions. They were going to see Times Square.

Bryan was getting a kick out of Sara. She was giving them directions and telling them about New York City, the Radio Music Hall, and the lights. She was excited about showing them the city because it was their first time. The traffic was heavy, but according to Sara, weekdays were the worse. Most workers lived outside the city.

Sara and Julie wore comfortable shoes. They would walk blocks after parking the car. They had made plans to eat lunch in the theatre district, but no play or musical on that trip. Bryan wanted to come again and go to Radio Music Hall with Julie.

"I want to walk in Macy's, not to buy anything, but look."

"Also, there are neat boutiques for looking," said Sara.

Sara told them not to appear as a tourist. Don't make eye contact. Look as if you know where you are going.

The lunch was good and fun too. Watching people, listening to them talking—Julie enjoyed everything about the city. It was hard for her not to make eye contact.

The afternoon was coming to an end. Macys was large and had many things to see. They had something to drink. Julie and Sara checked out the bathroom. They told Bryan the bathroom was very nice. He laughed.

After seeing Times Square at night, they planned to eat dinner after leaving the city.

Times Square didn't disappoint Julie. She was a country girl coming to the big city. The mood of the city changed at night. Bryan was holding tight to Julie's hand.

People moved, traffic moved, but Julie was standing still. The lights at Times Square amazed her. Sara moved to her side.

"What do you think?"

"I'm so glad we came. I have never seen anything like this." Bryan gave her hand a squeeze.

Walking back to the car, Bryan asked, "Sara, you okay?"

"Yes, Bryan. I have enjoyed the afternoon."

After stopping for dinner, it was getting late, and everyone was ready for home.

"Good night, Sara. Thank you."

"No, thank you, Julie, for letting me tag along. Bryan, you are a good driver."

"Thanks, Sara. Good night."

Bryan and Julie fell on the bed, tired but happy.

"Country went to the big city, didn't we?" Bryan said, hugging Julie.

"Yes, we did." Bryan loving her made her happy.

* * *

It was the first of July, and they wanted to go to Atlantic City. They would wait until after the fourth. They planned to leave early and watch the sun come up.

Watching the sun slowly coming into view with so many colors on their day trip to Atlantic City was pretty. They stopped at the park, enjoying their coffee and watching the sun rise.

"God can paint a pretty picture, don't you think so?"

"Yes, Julie have I told you that I love you?"

"Not today. I love you, Bryan. Will you pray that God will continue to bless our marriage and keep us safe today?"

"Yes."

Listening to Bryan's prayer was a blessing to Julie. She wanted a Christian husband, and God answered her prayer. *Thank you, Father.*

The sun was in full view.

"Ready?"

"Yes."

Atlantic City was the host of Miss America pageant, boardwalk, shops, and the ocean. She was excited.

Their day was filled with walking, laughing, eating, and shopping. They were teenagers again.

"Don't worry. Be happy." That was who they were. What a day!

The next week, Bryan came home from the base, and he had news.

"What?"

"We are going home the first week of August. They are letting us go from full time to reserves.

"I am glad. This has been fun, but I want to see our house and my beauty shop. Are you ready for the telephone company?"

"I'm more than ready. I want us to go to New York. I will get tickets for Radio Music Hall. This will be our anniversary gift. Do you like that sound of that?" He picked her up and kissed her.

"I want to go to New York one more time. To see a show at Radio Music Hall will be a great anniversary gift. Rockefeller Center will be fun too."

There was not many days left in New Jersey. Julie wanted to make more memories—style Sara's hair, lunch with her, and hang out with Joe. She had told Sara they were leaving. Today she would see Joe and tell him.

So many things she was able to do while living on that beautiful street and state. She was thinking of these things as she walked to see Joe.

Joe was with a customer. She put change in the machine, lifted her Pepsi, and took the lid off with the opener on the side. The customer left, and Joe smiled and said hello.

"Joe, Bryan and I are leaving the first of August."

"That's too soon. I will miss you. Let's go outside."

He was a nice kind man. Julie would miss him too. They walked, neither one talking. She noticed birds, butterflies, and flowers. The trees were nice with the summer heat.

"Joe, do you like Sara?"

"Yes, she is a friend."

"Have you ever asked her out for dinner?"

"No, I have been to her house for dinner. That was when she had a dinner party. We were never alone."

"Why don't you call her? Ask her to have dinner with you. Take her somewhere nice. You know she is lots of fun."

"I would feel uncomfortable."

"You will be taking a friend to dinner. Will you call her before I leave?"

"Julie, you are hard to say no to. I'll think about."

"I style her hair on Thursday. Thursday would be the right night."

"Okay, I'll call her today."

She took his hand and smiled. She walked away, saying to herself, "Yes!"

The day after, she was having lunch with Sara. She wanted to know everything—the call, the answer, everything. She loved Sara and didn't want to think of her alone. Joe needed Sara. He was lonely.

The next day they had lunch at the Tea House. After Julie and Sara placed their orders, Sara smiled.

"What?"

"I have something to tell you. Joe called me yesterday."

"Oh."

"He surprised me. He wanted to take me to dinner."

"And what did you say?"

She laughed. "I said yes."

"When are you going?"

"Thursday night."

"I like Joe. You will have fun."

"You think so?"

"I know it. It's just two friends that care about each other so relax and enjoy yourself."

"Julie, it's a date."

She couldn't help herself; she laughed. "I know it's a date. You and I had a date for lunch today. Don't over think it. Talk, eat, and maybe a short walk after dinner. What do you think?"

"If the night is cool, I would like a walk."

They ate lunch. Julie saw Sara's eyes smiling.

She enjoyed her lunch, but hearing the "date" news made her day.

* * *

On Thursday, she told Sara, "After you dress for dinner, I will touch up your hair."

She wanted to see her dressed for her date.

She heard a knock on the door. It must be Sara. There she was, pretty in a crisp cotton dress with shoes to match.

"Sara, you are pretty. Come in."

Julie got her comb and mirror. Her hair needed very little touch up. Did Sara have on eye makeup? Yes, she did! It was a shade of green to match her dress and eyes.

"Are you excited?"

"I'm not sure what you call these feelings I have. Do you think I'll be sorry I said yes?"

"Absolutely not. Remember, you have known Joe for a long time."

"Thanks, Julie." She stood to leave and gave Julie a hug.

Julie didn't close the door completely. She wanted to see Joe. The door bell rang, and Sara walked to the door.

"Hello, Joe."

"Hello, Sara. Are you ready? You look nice."

"Thank you. Let me get my purse."

They were gone, and Julie wished she could see them walking to the car. From her place, she couldn't see the front drive.

When Bryan came home, she told him about Sara and Joe.

"Is this the first time they have gone out together?"

"Yes."

"What did you do?"

"Me?" She laughed and walked to him.

"Yes, my love, you."

She told him everything, even about spying on them when Joe came for Sara.

"I'm glad they are out together. Maybe they needed a little push. Don't push any more. Okay?"

"Okay."

"I got our tickets for Radio Music Hall."

Julie was excited. "When are we going?"

"This will be our last Saturday here. We will make a day in New York. Sound like fun?"

"Yes, yes, yes." She would see the Rockettes.

Saturday and their day in New York came with a nice lunch and going to the RCA building. They went to the seventieth floor observatory deck, watching the show at Radio City Music Hall, and the stage rose from beneath the floor. After each performance, the stage would slowly disappear. It was great. The day was a dream for Julie. They finished the day at Times Square; they watched the lights and went to their apartment tired and happy.

Lying in bed, Julie said, unable to sleep, "Bryan, what a day!"

"Did you have fun?"

"Yes, I have memories to last forever. Thank you for this day."

"You are welcome. I enjoyed everything, but most of all, I enjoyed watching you. Julie, you make everything fun. I love you."

"I love you."

Sara made breakfast for Bryan and Julie. It was the day they'll leave New Jersey. The breakfast was a nice surprise.

Julie gave Sara her gift—a pin in the shape of a flower. She loved it.

Sara had tears in her eyes as they walked to the front door. Julie could feel the tears on her face. After hugging, exchanging "thank yous," "miss yous," and "please writes," their time with Sara was over.

Julie turned and looked at Sara and the house that had given her so much joy.

Bryan slowed the car at Joe's place but didn't stop. They had already said good-bye to him. He looked at Julie, but she was staring out her window.

"Julie, would you like something cold to drink?"

She turned and looked at him, "Yes."

"Don't be sad, Julie."

"I have mixed emotions, but I'm not sad. I feel blessed to have this time here."

After stopping for Pepsi, they were on their way to North Carolina.

Chapter 16

After returning from New Jersey, Julie wasn't expecting a baby. Her time away with Bryan was so much fun. They did not think or talk about a baby, but she hoped it would happen.

Their first stop was to see Julie's mom and dad. After hugging them, she asked, "Why didn't you write me?"

"We didn't have your address."

"I wrote you every week."

"There was no return address."

"I'm sorry." *Why didn't I put a return address? I wrote them and they knew I was okay. No return address.* She needed this time to completely relax, and God knew that.

She had written about different things she had seen and done, but they wanted to know more. Her mama and daddy were happy to see them. She could see pride in their eyes.

Bryan was out of active duty, so they would return to their previous life. Julie was ready to be in her beauty shop. Bryan was glad to be out of the army. He sang,

"I'm out of the army now." He would be in the reserves for one more year.

Being away from their house, they knew that the neighbors were keeping their eyes on it. Bryan had paid someone to mow their grass, but Julie wanted to see for herself. Two months had passed, and they were glad to be going home.

Home, their house, was built with love and hard work.

She jumped out of the car and ran to the back door. "Please hurry, Bryan."

He unlocked the door, and they went inside. She went from room to room.

"Everything is here. No one broke in, but I see dust on everything. Bryan!"

"Yes."

"Come to the front window. I have a surprise for you."

"Coming. What?"

She was looking out the window, and he walked over to her. She put her arms around his waist.

"Welcome home, my husband."

"Welcome home, my Julie."

"Let's walk around our yard." Everything was neat and growing. They sat at their picnic table under the pines.

"Bryan, we are so blessed."

"Yes, we are. You want to grill tonight? I can go to the butchers." The butcher would cut steaks the way Bryan liked.

"Steak, baked potatoes, and salad will be a nice dinner."

"Yes, I'll get everything."

"I'll unpack our things and make tea." After a quick kiss, he was gone.

Unpacking happily, she couldn't walk past the two empty rooms without stopping. She saw a little girl's room with dolls and a play kitchen. She saw a little boy's room with trucks and a toy box. There were cars, puzzles, and blocks, and he was sitting on the floor. "He looks like his daddy." The little girl had two cups on the table and pouring tea. Looking up with her blond hair, she smiled. "Come on, Mama." It was so real! She dropped to the floor. "I thank you, Father, for our future children."

She was finished when Bryan returned. All the dust was gone.

"Bryan, after dinner, I want to go to the salon."

"We will." He was getting the steaks ready for the grill. The potatoes were in the oven. Julie put the salad in the fridge and walked outside with Bryan. He loved grilling.

It was too hot to eat outside. They ate at their kitchen bar.

Julie put the dishes in the dishwasher.

"Ready?"

They were going to the salon. What would she find?

When Bryan opened the door and Julie walked inside, she was surprised. Everything was clean and shining. On the desk was a large arrangement of flowers. The flowers were from the customers with a note saying, "Welcome back. We missed you." Joann had left her a note. "We are glad you are home. I will see you Monday."

"Bryan, can you believe this? I don't deserve my customers, but I am thankful. Joann was the right person to manage the salon in my absence."

"You deserve this, Julie. You work hard and give customers more than they pay for."

She looked at the appointment book. Joann had marked Monday off for Julie. She was playing it safe and giving Julie time to get home. Tuesday was booked with haircuts and a perm for her.

"I'll take the flowers home and enjoy them Sunday and Monday. I will bring them back on Tuesday. Let me check the stock room, and we will go."

Her perm she needed for Tuesday was in stock. She knew Fayetteville had a beauty supply house for salons.

She was tired and ready for her bed.

"Ready?"

"Yes, you will sleep well tonight, knowing your salon is the way you left it."

"Yes, I will. Let's go."

* * *

After being home for a month, Julie was concerned that she was not pregnant. The temperature chart didn't work. Her doctor was hoping that reducing stress and not focusing on getting pregnant would help. New Jersey proved that didn't work. She made an appointment to see her ob-gyn.

Her periods were more painful, and she shared that with the doctor. Further testing at the hospital was recommended for Julie, and Bryan was to see a doctor. They were hoping for an answer.

After three months, Julie went to see her doctor. He had asked her to come. They knew Bryan had a low sperm count. She was hoping her doctor would have a positive answer.

"Julie, I'm glad you came in," said Dr. Sawyer. "After reviewing your test…I'm sorry, you have endometriosis."

Julie stared and said nothing.

"Do you know what endometriosis is?"

"No."

He opened a book on his desk and showed her a picture.

"This is endometriosis, making it almost impossible for you to conceive. You have the advanced stage. In the future, you may need surgery. I'm sorry." He told her how it happens and the results.

"I want you to read about your condition. I'll leave you alone. My nurse will come and check on you. I am sorry."

Julie stared at the picture and began to read. Her heart was beating fast, and she tried to calm herself. "No baby. I can't have a baby!" After some time, the nurse came in.

"Are you all right, Julie?"

"Yes. Thank you." She stood up and wanted to run but made herself walk.

Bryan was waiting in the car. The tears were falling as she walked to the car. He opened the door for her.

She didn't move after getting into the car. Her hands locked together.

"I can't have a baby."

"We will adopt. We will have a baby."

"I'm sorry."

"I'm sorry too." The doctor had told Bryan it would be hard for him because of his sperm count.

Julie was sobbing. Her body was shaking, and she wanted to scream. She thought, "*Don't let him touch me. Where are you God?*" The crying stopped, and she wiped her face. Like the calm after a storm, she was calm.

"Adopt?"

"Yes, we will adopt."

What is the first step? She thought, "*I will call my doctor.*"

Lying in bed that night, she tried to come to terms with what was happening. As time passed, she had only been pregnant one time. Deep down inside they knew the only answer for them would be adoption. God wanted them to wait for an answer and be ready to accept it. She wanted to have a long talk with Bryan before calling Dr. Sawyer.

Bryan's mother had a sister who adopted a baby boy. He was two years younger than Bryan. No one ever thought about him being adopted. He was one of the cousins.

They talked and cried. *Will we have a baby boy or baby girl?* Bryan said, "Maybe a girl?" He had a brother. One decision made. Julie knew she would love having a girl, then a boy. Bryan laughed at that—Julie planning for a girl and a boy. She knew her doctor would have the information on who to contact about adoption. Dr. Sawyer's associate had two adopted children. He had shared that with Julie one day when she had questions about having a baby. Monday would be the first day of bringing a baby girl home—to their home!

Chapter 17

They were planning a long weekend with Will and Hilda. They were going to the mountains of North Carolina. They would go through Ashville to Chimney Rock and Cherokee.

The mountain area in the fall with pretty colors would give Julie something to think about. She had to be patient about the adoption. She wanted to share with Hilda their plans for a baby girl.

Bryan wanted to drive, and they would share expenses. He didn't like sitting in the passenger's side, watching someone else drive.

The day to leave was here. They drove to Will and Hilda's house. Their bags were in the trunk with Julie and Hilda in the back seat; they were on their way. The four went to the same church, and everyone had different jobs. Sharing would be nice.

Outside of Ashville, they stopped for lunch and bathroom break. With Hilda, Julie was a teenager again, young and no responsibilities for a short time.

The mountains didn't disappoint them. God had painted shades of yellow, bronze, orange, and red. They passed waterfalls, went around sharp turns, and sometimes saw a bear; they were having fun. Signs like "Watch for falling rocks" made Bryan cautious with his driving.

With no reservations, they were looking for a place to sleep. There was a sign with cabins to rent. Bryan said, "Do you want to stop?" Everyone said yes. There was a lake behind the cabin, and they decided to stay together. There was a bathroom between the bedrooms and a small kitchen. They paid and walked outside. It was a pretty view from the porch.

Will wanted to find a restaurant and everyone agreed.

They were only ten miles from Cherokee. A restaurant was close to the cabins. It was a log building, and inside was pretty. There were table cloths with a small lantern on each table, and the light gave a soft glow. There were also wagon wheel lights from the ceiling and country music.

Julie said, "Bryan, may I have this dance?"

"I don't think so."

Everyone laughed.

Their dinner was barbecue, slaw, fries, and hush-puppies. The ice tea was good. They took slices of pie for later.

They played cards at the kitchen table and later pie and coffee on the porch with the stars and the moon shining on the lake.

Next day at Cherokee, watching the Cherokee Indians make baskets, pottery, and the dolls were amazing. Dolls from corn shucks, baskets made of white oak, river cane, and honeysuckle. Handmade items were their livelihood. Each craft was learned from generation to generation. Julie and Hilda couldn't decide between pottery and a basket. They decided on pottery.

Julie was able to share with Hilda about wanting a baby. Will and Bryan were having a Pepsi. Hilda said she thought they were waiting until the house was finished but didn't think about a problem to conceive. Tears were falling on Julie's face, and Hilda gave her a hug. She told Hilda about plans to adopt a baby.

They drove further and saw roadside stands with apple cider near the road. Bryan wanted cider so they stopped.

Further down the road, they saw water running downstream over rocks. It was a pretty spot to stop. Julie and Hilda took their shoes off, having fun stepping from rock to rock. Will and Bryan said next time they would bring their fishing polls. They saw a few fish.

Will said, "Are you children ready to go?"

"Yes, daddy," said Julie and Hilda, and they laughed.

The mountain trip was a nice break. Her customers heard about the trip but would know nothing about their baby girl until Julie saw her. She would share with them the date they would bring her home. She had no doubt God had a baby for them.

* * *

Julie got the information needed to make an appointment to begin the adoption. She and Bryan would meet Ms. Mayer for their interview. She was very nervous. It was important to make a good impression. A birth mother gave up her baby to have a better life. They wouldn't disappoint Ms. Mayer or the mother.

When Julie walked into Ms. Mayer's office, she wanted to like her. She looked at her eyes when she introduced herself.

Bryan said, "This is Julie and I am Bryan."

"Welcome, Bryan and Julie." Her eyes and mouth were smiling.

Julie relaxed but held Bryan's hand.

Ms. Mayer wanted to know about the reason for adoption. Julie told her about the doctor's appointments and the final one.

"I'm sorry, Julie."

She wanted to know about Julie and Bryan, their careers, where they lived, their families, and if their family would accept adopting a baby.

Filling out the application and feeling completely drained, they stood to go. The next meeting would be at their house. Julie liked Ms. Mayer.

Julie looked at Ms. Mayer and said, "Thank you."

"You are welcome, Julie. See you soon."

They rode home in silence. Julie walked through the back door and went to their bedroom. Putting her head on the bed and on her knees, she prayed. With tears, she asked God for strength and to take care of their baby girl. She stood up, and Bryan took her in his arms.

Chapter 18

Y ou can't put life on hold. Julie had her beauty shop, and Bryan had the telephone company. They were busy with church, work, and friends. It was hard not to dwell on the "what ifs." They had to wait until the next appointment and then what? It was a walk of faith and knowing God was in control. Was it easy? No.

After three weeks, Ms Mayer made an appointment to go to their house. They made it on Julie's day off. She said it wasn't necessary for Bryan to be there.

The home appointment was Tuesday. Julie didn't know what to expect. The yard was neat and no dust in the house. She made ice tea and waited for Ms. Mayer. Thirty minutes to go.

She was here. Julie opened the door.

"Come in."

"Hello, Julie. Your yard is nice."

"Thank you. Do you want me to show you the house and our baby's room?"

"Yes, please."

They walked down the hall toward the first room on the left. Julie walked into the empty room.

"This will be our baby girl's room. The crib will go on this wall. We will have a rocking chair here and plenty of room for her to play as she grows."

"Your house is pretty. Any little girl would love this room."

Julie walked to the next room on the left.

"This will be our little boy's room."

Ms. Mayer noticed the window treatments in the girl and boy's room was already in place.

"Their bath is here." It was at the end of the hallway.

"The master bedroom and bath is across from our children's rooms."

Going to the family room, they passed the dining room and kitchen. Ms. Mayers saw the empty living room when she came through the front door.

Ms. Mayer opened the back door and looked outside.

"Julie, how large is your property?"

"We have one acre. Would you like some ice tea?"

"No thanks. I am pleased and surprised. A little girl would love growing up here. When the paper work is complete, we will search for your baby girl."

"That's great news. I know you don't know how long, but maybe the average wait."

"You should have your baby girl within a year. Thank you, Julie."

"Thank you. We will wait to hear from you."

She was gone, and Julie let out a loud yes. She called Bryan and told him.

"No more visits?"

"No. Not until we meet our new baby girl."

"Julie, breathe. Our prayers are answered."

She was having a hard time calming down.

"Okay, I'm fine and very happy."

"I love you, Julie."

"I love you." She hung up the phone and walked to her baby girl's room. *I will have a tough time waiting to see you and hold you.* Tears were falling on Julie's face.

The next day, she called Hilda and asked if she would like to go shopping. Julie wanted to go to Small Town, a store with everything for babies and small children—furniture, clothes, and lots of toys for their baby girl.

"Hilda, I know I have months, but I have made myself stay away from this store. I'm not going to buy anything. We can have lunch."

"I would love to go. You want to leave around 10:00 a.m. on Saturday?"

"Yes, I'll pick you up."

At the store everything was organized. The cribs, how many do they have? Julie had a pad and pen to write style and prices of the big pieces. She knew the next time may be different choices. Everything was so pretty.

"Hilda, this is the crib."

"Are you sure?"

"Yes. White, classic, and our little boy will able to use it too."

"How many years will you wait for your baby boy?"

"Three to four years."

Julie touched clothes and toys. She was having fun getting ideas on a take-home outfit.

"Okay, Hilda, are you ready for lunch?"

"I'm ready if you are."

Their lunch was fun. Their talk was about Christmas. Julie noticed Hilda didn't talk about her and Will having a baby. For years, she didn't talk about that subject either.

She told Bryan about the crib. The owner told them to allow three weeks after ordering. They wouldn't order until they hear from Ms. Mayer.

* * *

Will played golf. Bryan tried it, but he didn't like it. Julie and Hilda decided to learn. They laughed a lot but would not let the game beat them. Or would they? One day they played with Will. Making a bad play, he threw his club at a tree.

Hilda said, "Do you see why I don't play with him?"

Julie could see why

Bryan enjoyed his small boat. He and Julie learned to water ski. Will and Hilda wanted no part in that. Faye, the pastor's wife, enjoyed boating but no skiing. Bryan, Julie, Mark, Faye, and their little boy, Randy, enjoyed the lake together. They had a boat for fishing.

Julie told Faye about adoption and their baby girl. She wanted their prayers.

"I'm so excited for you. You are going to make a great mom."

"Thank you."

She was thinking about names. What would sound good with Mills? They had to decide. Her mom's name was Marie and Bryan's mom name was Lucille. Definitely there would be no Marie or Lucille for their baby's name. *We will choose two names and when we see her, we will know.*

Chapter 19

C hristmas came along with Bryan and Julie's birth-
days, but there was no news about their baby.
Everyone said have fun because it will be all about the
baby when they bring her home. Julie liked the sound
of that—all about her baby.

Ms. Mayer called and asked them to go and see a
pretty baby girl. The night before they were to go, Julie
couldn't sleep. They had waited so long for a baby.

When Ms. Mayer put the baby into Julie's arms and
she looked at her tiny face, the love that overwhelmed
her was surprising. She knew it would be easy to love a
baby, but this was a mother holding her—her mother.
The baby's eyes with long eyelashes fixed on her. Julie
was laughing and crying.

"You are beautiful, tiny, tiny baby girl." She put her
finger into the little hand, and the baby was holding
tight. Julie forgot everyone but her baby. Bryan had
touched the other hand of their baby. Julie looked at
him, and he was smiling.

"Well, what do you think?" asked Ms. Mayer.

Julie said, "May we take our baby girl home?"

"Later." She told them the waiting period before the
babies could go to their new home.

"What will happen to her until then?"

"Julie, we will take very good care of her."

"I don't want to leave her."

"I understand, but you have to wait a few more weeks."

Julie was crying when Ms. Mayer took their baby. Bryan took her in his arms. She saw tears in his eyes.

"A few more weeks," he whispered.

Ms. Mayer returned and told them again that their baby girl would be in good hands. "Five more weeks, and I'll call you."

"Is it okay to order the crib? We need three weeks when placing the order."

"Yes, I feel sure everything will be final in five weeks. Do you have a lawyer?"

Bryan told her yes and that the papers were ready for the details.

"Great, I will call you. Thank you for coming in."

"Thank you for helping us. Can you tell us about the birth mother?"

"Julie, the most I can tell you is the mother is a special woman. She wants a loving home for her baby. When I told her about the couple that might adopt her baby, she was thankful." She also told them a little about the mother's background, disease, etc. The privacy of the mother was important.

Leaving their baby girl was the hardest thing Julie had ever experienced.

"Julie, would you like to go to Small Town?"

"Yes, I want to select her outfit. I want her to wear it home. She is so tiny. Ms. Mayer said she weighed six pounds."

They left the store with a pretty dress and the smallest shoes they had. Julie was holding the shoes in her hands as they drove home. They would need other things but not today. *Anna Rae, do you think these shoes will fit?*

"Bryan, have we decided on Anna Rae for our baby girl's name?"

"Yes, she is Anna Rae."

* * *

Her dad and mama came for a visit. Hearing that her dad was no longer drinking alcohol was great news. It had been over a month, and he was involved in a church. They needed work done on the pastor's house, and he was helping. It was a miracle.

They thought the baby's room was pretty. It was ready with a crib, changing table, lots of stuffed animals, and a rocking chair to rock Anna.

Julie showed them the outfit Anna would wear home. Her mama wanted to know the day.

"In one week. We got the call on Friday."

They had to take the legal papers and Anna's outfit.

Julie's friend Hilda and her friend Faye, the pastor's wife, would give her a shower on Sunday afternoon. It would be at Faye's home. She had been to baby showers where the mom had a huge stomach, but she wasn't pregnant. She was pleased but didn't know what to expect.

The shower was fun. Julie was expecting a baby! The games, food, gifts, and so many women from their church came. Hilda and Faye were special friends.

The news was out at the salon. They gave gifts, and she opened each one. She didn't know there were so many different outfits for a baby girl. Some gave gift cards. Julie was counting her blessings.

Julie would go into the baby's room and sit in the rocking chair.

"Anna, this is your room."

Christmas would be more fun with their baby. She would be five months then.

Chapter 20

Julie got up early and dressed. She knew they wouldn't leave for another two hours. Bryan had taken the day off. He would have Friday, Saturday, and Sunday with their baby girl. Anna was so tiny, but they were told that she was a healthy baby.

"Julie, what are you doing?" She was at the crib, staring. "The bed is big."

"She will grow, and then it won't look so big."

"Will I make a good mother?"

"You know the answer. You will make a great mother. I want to take you to breakfast."

"Okay."

The drive into Fayetteville was a quiet one, each with their thoughts.

Julie's breakfast was one half grapefruit and whole-wheat toast with coffee. Bryan had eggs, bacon, grits, and biscuits with coffee. He was slim, but she knew this was a big breakfast for him.

"Honey you hungry?"

"Yes, I think it might be excitement."

"I am ready to bring Anna home. You think she will be dressed in her new outfit?"

"Ms. Mayer said she would have her dressed and ready for us."

They walked into Ms. Mayer's office, and she was smiling.

"Your baby girl is ready to go home with her mama and daddy." She picked up the phone and said, "Anna's parents are here."

Julie was so excited to see their baby all dressed and ready to go.

Anna was laid in her arms.

"Hi, Anna, I missed you."

Bryan put his arm around Julie's shoulders and touched Anna with his other hand.

"Isn't she pretty, Daddy?"

"Yes, look at her eyes and lashes. Let's go home, Anna."

"Thank you for taking care of our baby."

Bryan said, "Thank you," and shook Ms. Mayer's hand.

Julie sat in the car with Anna over her legs so she could see her face. The tears were falling.

Anna's shoes were off. Julie touched the little feet with socks and laughed.

"We purchased the smallest shoes the store had, and they are too big."

At home, Bryan went around the car and opened Julie's door. He took Anna, and they went into the nursery.

She can't believe how comfortable Bryan was holding their baby girl. They looked at each other, smiling.

"Anna, you like your daddy?" She smiled, and that was a yes. "Come to mama, Anna. I need to change you." Bryan let down the crib side and Julie laid her down.

"Let's take that dress off and put something comfortable on you. Do you like your bed?" Anna didn't take her eyes off Julie. "I'm going to pull your dress over your head. Where is Anna? I see you."

After changing her, Julie and Anna rocked in the rocking chair.

"Bryan, we haven't heard her cry."

"She's too happy to cry." He was at her knees, looking at his two girls.

Anna was on schedule with her bottle, and at 2:00 a.m., Julie was more than glad to hold her. Watching her enjoy her milk, she said, "Thank you, Father." God had chosen Anna's family.

Bryan and Julie were glad he had chosen them. She looked up, and Bryan was standing at the door.

"Are my girls okay?"

"Yes."

Anna's eyes were closing. She was almost finished with her milk. Her eyes then opened. "Hi, Anna, are you ready to sleep?" Her eyes closed. Julie stood up and said, "I love you."

"I don't think I will ever get tired of watching you sleep." She laid her hand on Anna's stomach. "Good night."

Bryan and Julie walked to their bed, and on their knees, thanked God for Anna. "Please keep her safe and well."

Four years later, Bryan and Julie brought their son Bryan Allen home. Julie told Ms. Mayer she wanted a baby boy that looked like Bryan. It was amazing; he did.

Julie was excited to have their son. Watching him grow would be another miracle that God was giving them. His eyes with long lashes could melt his mama's heart. She said, "He's a pretty baby." Bryan said, "Don't say pretty, good-looking maybe."

Anna Rae looked in Allen's crib and said, "He can't do anything." He was not a playmate for her yet, but being Mama's helper was fun.

They received gifts from their family, friends, and Julie's customers for their son. Anna received gifts too. Allen seemed to enjoy all the attention.

Julie's friends Hilda and Will Bradford adopted a son. He came home with them two months after Julie and Bryan's son. The boys became friends.

Dear Readers

I hope you know my God, the only God. He created us and loved us so much that he sent his son, Jesus, to die for our sins. Jesus arose on the third day. We can have a relationship with God through our faith in Jesus Christ.

Adoption is an answer to prayers for couples who are unable to conceive. God creates each child. Let your unborn baby live.